NOVA DRAGON

BOOK ONE OF THE GOBLIN STAR

By Gama Ray Martinez

* Forthcoming

NOVA DRAGON

BOOK ONE OF THE GOBLIN STAR

GAMA RAY MARTINEZ

Tolwis

ISBN: 1-944091-10-6

ISBN-13: 978-1-944091-10-1

CHAPTER 1

Mistress Elawn focused her emerald eyes on Radek. The elven teacher tapped her foot on the ground, and he could feel the rest of the students staring at him. He could almost hear them whispering 'stupid human' behind his back. They probably would've answered the question already, if she had asked them. He scratched his shoulder. He still wasn't used to the heavy brown robes the elves wore to school. He didn't understand why a race advanced enough to build a space station between the stars of a binary system couldn't figure out how to make clothes that didn't itch. The teacher raised an eyebrow, and he forced himself to stop scratching. He tried to remember. The answer was right on the tip of his tongue.

"Dwarves carve runes in stone. Elves sing to crystals. Humans chant to empower wood in the shape of staves or wands. Goblins..." He searched his memory. "Goblins shape gold?"

The students laughed, and Radek felt his face heat up. Mistress Elawn cleared her throat, and the class went silent.

"Goblins use bone magic. Shaped gold was used by dragons before they retreated from known space. Certain of their artifacts still use it. Dwarves have some aptitude there as well, which is why they so often utilize dragon relics. It's an example of cross species magic, but if goblins tried to build a star drive powered by gold, they would end up scattering their molecules across half a light year."

The crystals at the front of the room chimed and alternated between blue and green. Mistress Elawn waved a hand and sang a word that faded from Radek's memory almost instantly. The crystals dimmed. She walked to the front of class, her feet barely disturbing the illusion of grass covering the floor.

"For tomorrow, look at the files on cross species magic, particularly on what types of magic each of the major races can use." A pudgy boy with a golden link hanging from his left ear raised his hand. He snickered and looked at Radek. Mistress Elawn didn't even glance at the student. "Yes, Fanul, that includes humans. You'll give a ten-minute speech on the unique human ability to integrate the magic of other races into their own."

Fanul lowered his hand and glared at Radek, as if it had been his fault. Mistress Elawn raised a hand, and the students inclined their heads. Some sang a few words, and their belongings deposited themselves in their bag, but Radek had to gather his by hand. They all stood and filed out of the classroom. Radek was the last to finish packing up his things. He rolled up a scroll and shoved it into his bag before standing to leave.

"Don't let them bother you, Radek," Mistress Elawn stumbled over his name, incorrectly emphasizing the second syllable as she would for an elven name. "Even elves can be cruel when they're children."

He sighed and nodded. 'Even elves' as if elves couldn't be just as mean as humans. They liked to pretend they were better than everyone else, but according to his father, the first human ambassador on the elven space station *Vanel*, elves could be just as selfish and stubborn as anyone else. Radek didn't say any of that, though. Instead, he just smiled.

"Yes, Mistress Elawn. I'll remember that."

"Good, and work on your song. Just because you can't become a full singer doesn't mean you shouldn't learn enough to pick up your supplies."

He turned away as he felt his face heat up. It was useless to say he'd been working on his song for months and still hadn't been able to do so much as light a candle. Regardless of the fact that his father's files said a human should be able to learn at least a little elf magic, he just didn't seem to have the knack for it.

"Yes, Mistress Elawn." He slung his bag onto his shoulder. "Can I go now?"

"Of course. I'll see you tomorrow."

Radek walked out of the classroom and into the hall. Blue shafts of sunlight shone through a canopy of trees, and a cool breeze carried the scent of pine to his nose. It wasn't really pine, of course. A certain type of grass from the elven home world, with a name Radek couldn't pronounce, smelled almost exactly like pine, and they liked to use it in the illusions they created to decorate the space station.

He strode down the forest path, trying to ignore the looks the elves gave him. It didn't help that he was as tall as most elven adults, who rarely grew taller than five feet. He kept his head down as the path wound around a corner that had been made to look like an oak tree. Suddenly, one of the roots rose up and wrapped itself around his ankle. He yelped as he fell, and though the ground might look like grass, it still felt like metal when he slammed into it. He looked up to see a group of students pointing and laughing. He glanced down. The root had released him and was, once again, immobile next to the tree.

He glared at them as they ran off. He wasn't even sure how they'd managed to trip him with an illusion, but then, he barely understood even the most basic principles of elven magic.

"I miss Treya," he said under his breath.

His father had been governor of Treya, the first human colony outside of the Sol system. Radek had friends there. They'd all been excited to build a home on a new world, but then the goblins had attacked the elves, and had plunged that part of the galaxy into war. The humans had eventually joined with the elves, and once the war was over and the Rageshian Treaty signed, the elves had invited the humans to send an ambassador to the space station *Vanel*. Radek didn't understand the politics involved, but his father had been chosen, and they had come here. Now Radek had to go to class and help be a bridge between humans and elves, whatever that meant.

He sighed and picked himself up off the ground. As soon as he was on his feet, something crashed into him from behind, and he fell onto his stomach as the thing pressed onto his back.

"Oh, sorry," a voice said from atop him, and a weight was lifted off.

Radek stood again and turned around. An elven child, no older than Radek himself, though shorter by nearly a foot, stared up at him. He wore the traditional student's robes, but they were torn and covered in oil stains as well as a few other substances Radek couldn't identify. He had dirt in one ear and his sandy hair went out in all directions, making him look like a bush as much as anything else. Of course all elves were actually plants, but most didn't look like it. The elf's gray eyes went wide.

"Oh, I thought you were an adult. You're the human kid, aren't you?"

Radek stood up straight. "Yes. I'm Radek."

The elf started to incline his head but stopped after a second and held out his hand. Radek blinked at it for a second. He took it, and they shook.

"I'm Kukak. That's my human name."

Radek stared at him. "That's not a human name."

"Sure it is. It has the 'ck' sound, just like yours."

"That's not what makes a human name."

The elf looked up at the ceiling, the elven version of shrugging. "It's close enough."

"Why don't you tell me your elf name?"

The elf smirked. "Why don't *you* tell me *your* elf name?"

"I don't have an elf name."

"Why not? I have a human one."

"No you don't. You just put together a bunch of sounds."

The elf let out a breath. "That's what human names are."

"No, they're not."

He looked at the ceiling again. "If you say so. So what's your elf name?"

Radek stared at him for a second before sighing. "Lalon."

The elf raised an eyebrow. "That's not an elf name."

Radek clenched his teeth. "Why don't you tell me your elf name so I have a better example?"

"There are lots of people here who have elf names. You have plenty of examples. You should be able to come up with a better name than Lalon."

"Are you going to tell me your name or not?"

"I already did."

"Your elf name."

He looked at the ceiling. "Ovian. I'm going to the goblin enclave. Do you want to come?"

Even during the war, the goblins had maintained a presence here, and *Vanel* had often been used as neutral ground. They had kept their enclave even after being defeated. Radek looked around, but no one was close enough to hear. They seemed to be in an empty forest. There was even an illusionary animal that looked like a squirrel with two tails jumping from tree to tree.

"I thought the goblin enclave was off limits."

"Well, yes. If we were allowed there, it wouldn't be any fun."

"But..." Radek tried to think of a reason not to go, but almost everything he'd done since he'd gotten here had been boring or lonely or both. This was the first thing that wasn't. After a few seconds, he nodded. "Let's go."

CHAPTER 2

They walked down what seemed to be a winding forest path for a few minutes before reaching the end of the illusionary terrain which marked the border of the elven sector of the station. The silvery metal from which *Vanel* had been constructed gleamed in the lights inset in the ceiling. They moved quietly, with Ovian constantly peeking around corners to avoid being seen. Though they both wore soft leather boots, Radek's footsteps were much heavier than his elven companion, and he felt like the whole station must be able to hear, but they didn't attract undue attention.

They turned a corner into a particularly wide hall and peered down it. Two burly goblins stood in front of a large metal door. Nearly as tall as elves, they looked like they were made of pure muscle. Leathery skin stretched over their bodies, and they had pointed ears and bald heads. Their arms ended in six-clawed hands, and they carried a weapon that looked like a cross between an ax and a gun. There seemed to be carvings on the door, but they were too far for Radek to make out any details.

Ovian pulled Radek back around the corner. Then, he ran his hand along the wall until it clicked under his fingers. A panel came free revealing a dark monitor. It lit up as soon as Ovian touched it.

The elf ran one finger across the screen.

"What's that?" Radek asked.

"It's a repair console. Technicians use it to find problems with the station's systems."

Flowing letters appeared on the screen. Radek tried to read them, but he'd only just begun learning to read Elven, and the writing went by too quickly. Ovian tapped several letters, and a metal square on the ceiling slid aside. A ladder silently extended downward.

"How did you do that?"

Ovian looked at the ceiling. "It's not hard. You just have to know the right codes."

Radek quirked an eyebrow. "Where did you get the codes?"

Ovian smiled but didn't answer. He scrambled up the ladder and disappeared down some unseen corridor. Radek just stared after him. After a few seconds, Ovian poked his head out of the hole.

"Are you coming?"

Radek looked around to make sure no one could see. A dim part of his mind recognized that he shouldn't be doing this, but he was caught up in Ovian's exuberance. Radek nodded and climbed up. Ovian sang a few words and the ladder lifted itself. As soon as it was up all the way, the panel closed. All around them, crystals lit up, shedding a soft blue light. They were in a small access tunnel, less than three feet tall, that was parallel to the hall below. Ovian was already crawling in the direction of the goblin enclave and Radek scurried after him.

"What are we looking for?"

"I want to see them using bone magic."

Radek stopped. "That's it? They had a goblin come into our class to demonstrate it. Unless..." Radek eyed Ovian's ragged clothes. They seemed to have been well made once, though the cloth at the knees had been worn out. Given how used to crawling through maintenance corridors Ovian apparently was, that didn't really surprise Radek. Still…"Do you go to school?"

Ovian paused and turned around. His eyes constantly darted about as he tried to look into every shadow. "Of course I do, but the goblins that my tutors brought just showed me how they make smoke. I want to see them using real bone magic, like they do for their star drive. Come on."

"But…"

Ovian was already moving through the corridor. Radek looked over his shoulder at the place where he had come into this passage. For the first time, he thought he might be in over his head. He considered going back but the ground seemed solid, and he had no idea how to open the hatch, so he hurried after the elf. They went on for a few minutes, with crystals lighting up as they approached and dimming behind them. Other, smaller passageways branched off, but Ovian wove through them without slowing.

"How do you know where to go?" Radek asked.

"It's all on the station's blueprints."

"Aren't those secret?"

"Yes, a little." He turned down a corridor. "Come on. I think it's this way."

"You think?"

"I only looked at the plans for a few seconds. Their engineering chamber is near the center of their enclave. We have to be near that now." Suddenly, he stopped and tapped the floor. "I think this is it."

Ovian sang a few words, and a slit appeared on the ground before him. He peeked through it and almost instantly pulled back. A second later, a pale hand reached up into the corridor. They both moved back. Muffled voices came from below. Suddenly, the floor slid out from under them. Radek cried out. There was singing, and his fall slowed a little. They crashed into the floor, but it felt like they had only gone a few feet.

A tall man stood over him, towering over the elven guard he was with. The human's dark hair reached to his shoulders and he wore a bright red jacket over a white shirt. The goblin guards stood in front of the door to the enclave. Radek and Ovian had apparently gone in a big circle. The man cleared his throat, and Radek found himself wishing he had never followed Ovian.

"Hello, father."

CHAPTER 3

Radek's father practically dragged him back to the human enclave. Unlike the areas that had been given to the other races, their sector currently consisted only of a sleeping chamber for each of them and receiving room where his father had meetings with other ambassadors. By the time they got to Radek's room, he was sweating. His father hadn't said a word, and that was always a bad sign. The door slid open when it detected him, and his father pointed to one of the chairs at his small table. Radek sat and avoided meeting his father's gaze. The viewscreen hanging from the wall alternated between images of the white star, *Jalon,* and the yellow one, *Branul,* the two stars that *Vanel* was nestled between. A holo of Radek, his parents, and his grandparents sat on his dresser. It had been taken before his mother had died. Next to the image sat a stick of dark wood, a wand that Radek had never been able to empower. His father cleared his throat, and Radek looked at him.

"What were you doing in the access shafts?"

Radek averted his eyes. "Nothing."

"Nothing? You came very close to causing an interstellar incident. Do you have any idea what would've happened if you'd been caught inside the goblin enclave? Everything beyond the front door is goblin territory. You would've been subject to their laws. Do you know what they do to intruders?"

Radek shrugged. "Mistress Elawn says they don't really eat people."

"No, they just torture them for information."

"But I don't know anything."

He let out a long breath. "You are an ambassador's son. If you had been caught sneaking around their enclave, they never would've believed you were there innocently. Why did you go there? Who was the elf with you?"

Radek's words tumbled over each other. "He was just someone that bumped into me. He wanted to see a goblin star drive. You did tell me I need to make friends."

His father shook his head. "Radek, you go to class with some of the children of the most important elves in their kingdom. Why don't you spend your free time with them instead of some troublemaker? Who is he? Some technician's son?"

"I think so. We didn't really talk that much."

"I don't want you spending time with him. I'm in the middle of negotiations with both the goblins and the elves. If all goes well, we'll end with both a goblin bone drive and an elven world to colonize."

"But aren't there like a million worlds we could colonize?"

"There are plenty of habitable worlds, but resource-rich planets with a climate practically identical to Earth that are close enough to both Earth and Treya to make travel convenient are another matter. Halune could be ideal. Can you please try to stay out of trouble?"

Radek looked away. "All right."

Silence followed for a second. Then, he felt his father's hand on his shoulder. He looked up.

"This is hard for you, isn't it? Living here, I mean."

Radek was staring at the holo of his of his family before he realized what he was doing. He sighed and met his father's eyes. "It's not so bad."

His father smiled. "You're a terrible liar, though I suppose I shouldn't be complaining about that. I was very selfish, bringing you here. Your grandparents wanted you to stay at Treya."

Radek pushed back from the table. "No!" His father looked startled. "I mean I want to stay with you."

His father's wrist chimed, and an elven face appeared in his communicator.

"I'm sorry," he said. "It's the Veelan. I have to take this."

Radek nodded, and his father got up to leave. The door slid up for him, but before he passed through, he turned back to Radek. "As soon as these negations are done, I'll request a transfer back to Treya. I'm sure they can find something for me to do there. We'll talk about your punishment later."

In spite of that, Radek felt a smile form on his face at the prospect of going home. His father tapped his wrist and spoke into it just as the door slid closed behind him.

CHAPTER 4

"Lalon," a voice drifted from above. "Lalon, are you there?"

Radek opened his eyes and sat up in his bed, but the room was completely dark.

"Lights."

Crystals strewn about the ceiling illuminated. He was the only one in the room, and the indicator by his door said there was no one on the other side. He was about to lie back down and dismiss it as a dream when a panel slid open on the ceiling, and Ovian's head poked out, as if he was hanging upside down. When he saw Radek, his eyes widened. "I knew I'd get it this time."

"Did you call me Lalon?"

Ovian looked up at him. "It's your elf name."

"You said it wasn't an elf name."

"Well, you worked so hard on it. I thought I'd be nice and use it anyway."

Radek rolled his eyes. "Can you please go away? My father told me not to spend time with you."

"He just doesn't know me yet."

"No, he doesn't want me to mess up his chances to get a bone drive."

Ovian's eyes widened, and a grin appeared on his face. "Well, that's good news then. I know where we can get a bone drive, or at least the plans for one."

"I'm not going with you so we can get lost trying to sneak into the goblin enclave, again."

"We wouldn't get lost. I looked at the schematics again, and I know where we went wrong. Anyway, I'm not talking about the goblin enclave. They just brought in a damaged ship. It's sitting in one of the docking bays. The goblins insisted it be kept separate from the main bay while they repair it, but I know where it is. I can get us there without anyone seeing us."

"I'm not going to steal a bone drive off a goblin ship."

Ovian laughed. Hanging from the ceiling as he was, the sight almost made Radek laugh. "That's the best part," Ovian said. "We don't have to steal it. It's the bone drive that was damaged. That means they probably have plans programmed into the repair golems. We just have to get to them and use the password to unscramble their security. Then, we can get the plans for a bone drive without anyone knowing."

"I don't think getting the password will be so easy."

"I already have the password. Are you coming?"

"My father told me..."

"Your father wants a bone drive, right? You can get it for him without him having to deal with the goblins. No one likes working with them anyway."

"But..."

Radek tried to think of a response, but nothing came. In fact, Ovian was making a good point. His father only needed to finish these two negotiations, and they could go back to Treya. If he could get ahold of bone drive plans without the goblins knowing, they could go home that much quicker.

"All right. I'll go, but we can't take too long. I don't want my father to know."

"No one will see us. Trust me."

Ovian sang and a ladder lowered itself into Radek's room. He climbed into the corridor, and the hatch sealed behind him. As before, Ovian scurried through a series of passages, though this time, they were in there much longer. The elf moved quickly, seemingly unaffected by the need to crawl. Several times, he had to stop and wait for Radek. Every time he did that, he let out a heavy sigh. Radek tried to go faster, but it was no use. After a few minutes, he was sweating, and his knees ached.

"Are we almost there? You said this wouldn't take too long."

"No, I didn't. You said it wouldn't take too long. I said no one would see us. Anyway, it's just up ahead."

'Just up ahead' turned out to be another half hour of crawling through access passages. Given that these were only maintenance shafts, Radek was surprised at how clean they were. The place was like a maze, and Radek had no idea how Ovian kept track of it. Finally, Ovian sang and a panel slid open. A ladder lowered itself, and they climbed down in front of a wide door. A few seconds later, the ladder lifted, and the panel closed. Ovian tapped a nearby screen. It lit up, and he ran his fingers across it. The door hummed and opened, revealing a thing Radek had only seen in historical records.

The goblin ship had to be at least twenty feet long and looked vaguely arrow shaped. A walkway had been lowered from the bottom, providing access to the ship's interior, and whirring sounds came from inside. Short wings jutted out from the sides of the ship, each of which held three cylindrical bulges.

"Are those weapons?"

Ovian nodded. "It's just a transport, so it's not that heavily armed for a goblin ship. There are three laser cannons on each wing. A plasma projector on the front, and the exhaust canon can send out balls of superheated fuel."

Radek gaped. "That's it, right?"

"Yes." Ovian paused. "Well, there are internal defenses too, but I'm pretty sure those are disabled while they do their repairs."

"You're pretty sure?"

"Look, they have to disable them for the golems to go in fix it, right?"

"I thought the goblins were disarmed after they lost the war."

Ovian laughed. "You should've seen one before the disarmament. You see those slots on the tip of the wing? Those used to hold missile launchers. The plasma projector might be strong, but it's nothing compared to the fusion blasters we forced them to remove."

Radek's throat went dry. "What kind of internal defenses do they have?"

"I'm not really sure, actually."

Radek stared at the elf, but Ovian casually walked toward the ship. Radek jogged to catch up with him, though he couldn't take his eyes off the plasma projector.

"What if it's something like poison gas? That wouldn't bother the golems."

"No, whatever it is, it would be able to harm constructs. Otherwise, they wouldn't be able to defend against anyone who tried to use golems to board them. One time, I saw a golem that had been hit by dwarven internal defenses, and its whole head was melted. It could only walk in circles. Everyone keeps saying how good the goblins are with weapons, so their internal defenses have to be worse than that."

Radek narrowed his eyes. "You're not really making me feel better about this."

Ovian looked at the ceiling. "You didn't have to come."

Radek gaped at him, but the elf had already started walking again. Radek rushed after him. As soon as Ovian stepped on the walkway, they heard heavy footsteps clanking on the metal floor. A stone man appeared at the top of the walkway and started walking down. It was taller than either elf or human, so tall it had to hunch its shoulders to avoid banging its head on the bottom of the ship. It had the same pointed ears and canted eyes as elves, but its larger proportions made it look more devilish than graceful. Its face twitched as if it was alive, and even its stone clothes seemed to shift as it walked. Its steps made the walkway vibrate, and it stopped right in front of the two boys. It looked down at them, and its eyes glowed green. Radek took an involuntary step back.

"You are not authorized to be here." It had a hollow reverberating voice that made a shiver ran down Radek's spine.

"Access code venurai lanief arnaror ventalin," Ovian said. Then, he sang a few words that immediately vanished from Radek's memory.

The golem inclined his head. "Priority one code acknowledged."

It turned and started walking back up into the ship. Ovian ran up to it and touched its leg. The golem turned around, and Ovian held up one of the green crystals used for data storage.

"Give me the plans for the goblin bone drive."

The golem's eyes brightened. A smile appeared on Ovian's face, but it faded when the golem scooped him up in one arm. Radek gasped and turned to run, but he'd only gone a few steps when a stone arm wrapped itself around him and lifted him off the ground. Ovian was singing, but the golem seemed impervious to whatever magic the elf was trying to use. A shrill sounded through the docking bay, and a red light started flashing. Ovian shouted the access code again and again, but the golem ignored him. Radek banged his fists against the arm holding him, and the golem seemed to wince, but its face returned to an expressionless stare a moment later, leaving Radek with bruised hands.

"What's happening?" Radek asked.

"I don't know. That code should've given me full access."

The alarm continued to blare, and a dozen elven guards came through the door, each armed with the crystal tipped pikes used for heavy combat rather than the hand blasters station security normally wore. Ovian was trying to kick the golem, but the statue held him out too far to reach its body. The guards raised their pikes, and though the crystals didn't glow, Radek's blood went cold. A guard wearing a golden sun pin on his breast sang, and the golem put them face down on the ground. Radek looked up as Ovian scrambled to his feet.

"Thank you for freeing us from that golem," Ovian said. "It appears to be malfunctioning. We will go now, and leave you to deal with it."

He stood with his back straight and his chin held high. He sounded nothing like a mere technician's son. Some of the guards exchanged glances, but the leader shook his head, and the others kept their weapons raised.

"I'm afraid not, Veelani Ovian. The golem is programed to restrain anyone trying to steal state secrets from another government. I have no choice but to put you and your companion in a holding cell."

CHAPTER 5

They sat on a hard bench behind an invisible wall that looked out into a hall containing several other cells, most of them unoccupied. The elves hadn't bothered to disguise this room with their illusions, so every surface was the same silvery metal as the rest of the station. Even so, the prison area seemed gloomy. The guards had contacted both of their fathers, and it already felt like they'd been waiting forever. Radek stared at Ovian. The elf slumped on the bench and seemed to be drained of energy, looking nothing like what Radek would expect of an elven noble.

"The guard called you Veelani. You're the Veelan's son?"

Unlike humans, elves had hereditary titles. The Veelan was the elven ambassador and governor over the space station, a position that his oldest child, Ovian apparently, would eventually inherit.

Ovian nodded. "I overheard my father using his codes. I thought they could unlock anything." His face lit up. "Disable cell door. Access code venurai lanief arnaror ventalin."

He sang for a few seconds, but gave up when nothing happened. Slowly, he reached for the door, and a green spark erupted from where his hand touched the energy field. He cried out and pulled back, and Radek caught the faint smell of ozone.

"Maybe I shouldn't try that again."

Before Radek could respond, an elf walked in front of their cell. His robes shimmered from blue to purple and back again. He wore an earring, a silver chain connecting the top and bottom of his left ear. His hair was the same sandy color as Ovian's, though his was combed straight and reached halfway down his back. His eyes focused on Ovian, and for a second, he went perfectly still. Radek couldn't say why, but it made him think of a tree that wouldn't budge no matter how strong a storm it endured.

"What did you think you were doing?"

He spoke softly, and his voice reminded Radek of thunder rumbling just before a storm let loose. Radek stood up and tried to hold his head high, but his chin quivered, and he could only meet the other elf's face for a second.

"It wasn't Radek's fault."

"No, I don't imagine it was. You've gotten in enough trouble that I think it's more likely you dragged him into it."

There were heavy footsteps and a second later, Radek's father appeared. He'd thrown a coat on over his night robe and his hair seemed to be in tangles, a stark contrast to the well-kept appearance of the Veelan. He glared at Radek before turning to Ovian's father and inclining his head.

"Veelan Javin. I didn't realize that was your son."

"Ambassador Kenneth. Yes, after our meeting, I was informed of his attempt to get into the goblin enclave with your son. I apologize for not informing you of his identity." He inclined his head in return. A faint smile appeared on his face. "When I said I wanted us to develop closer ties, I did not envision our sons being locked up together."

"Nor did I, Veelan." He turned to Radek and scowled. "Didn't I specifically tell you not to start an interstellar incident with the goblins?"

Radek lowered his eyes. "I'm sorry."

"We're both sorry," Ovian said. "Can you just get us out of here?"

"I'm not sure I should," the Veelan said. "This is the second time in as many days you've come close to undoing all my work with the goblins. I'm trying to create a lasting peace here, and you're not helping. I think it might be beneficial to leave you in there for a while. Maybe then you'll learn your lesson."

"No!" Radek said, his mind filled with images of growing old in prison.

"He's just joking," Ovian said, though he didn't sound so sure. "Besides, we didn't really do anything wrong. It's not like we actually got in to the enclave, and the golem wouldn't give me the bone drive plans with your code."

"Of course not. Do you think any government would trust us if I could just order our constructs to hand over sensitive information? How did you get my codes anyway?"

"I found them." The Veelan's eyes narrowed and Ovian looked away. "I snuck into your room through the access shafts. I listened when you unlocked the crystal chamber for the repair team a few days ago."

"I warded my voice when I did that."

Ovian shrugged. "The entrance to the access shaft is right above the door. You made your ward too big so I was inside of it."

Javin smirked. "I'll have to be more careful and keep closer tabs on you."

"Are the goblins going to take issue with this?" Radek's father asked.

The Veelan looked at the ceiling. "They might, but my son has a valid point. Since they didn't get into the ship, they never actually crossed into goblin territory. The only laws they broke were elven ones, and those, we can deal with. It'll probably damage your negotiations, but unless you want to hand your son over to the goblins, there's little you can do about that."

His father's expression brightened. "Do you think handing him over would help?"

"Father!"

"I did warn you."

Radek sputtered for a second until he saw the smile on his father's face. Then, he scowled.

"That's not funny."

"I could always ask the Veelan to leave you in the cell for a day or two."

"That's not funny either."

His father smiled. "Yes it is."

Chapter 6

What am I going to do with you?" Radek's father asked.

His father had spent most of the morning in a meeting with the Veelan and the Krom, the title given to the goblin ambassador. Radek had been forced to stay in his room, even to the point of missing class. His meals had been brought to him, though both lunch and dinner had been nothing but a thin vegetable soup. He'd wrinkled his nose at the earthy taste common to all elven dishes. It had been almost evening when his father had finally returned. There were dark circles under his eyes, and he seemed very tired. Radek started talking before his father had sat down.

"I thought if I could get the plans to a bone drive, all you would have to worry about was getting the planet."

"You didn't think there would be a problem if you stole it?"

"Ovian said it would be fine since we were just getting the plans from a golem and not actually stealing the drive."

"And you didn't see a problem with that?"

Radek looked away. "Maybe a little."

His father sighed. "I think I'm going to send you home."

"Father, no!" Radek met his father's gaze.

His father raised a hand and spoke in that quiet voice that was even more intimidating than his shouts. "Do you realize what you could've done? If you had succeeded, the goblins might well have declared war on us. Goodness knows they wouldn't need much provocation." His father shook his head. "They nearly defeated the elves. We wouldn't stand a chance."

"I'll stop. I promise. I'll stay away from the goblins."

His father raised an eyebrow. "Why are you so anxious to stay? I thought you hated this place."

Radek shrugged. "It's not so bad."

"It's not so bad since you found a friend, you mean."

"You said I should make friends with some of the children of important elves. Ovian is the Veelan's son."

"He's a troublemaker, and the trouble he causes doesn't just affect you."

For a moment, Radek stared at his reflection in the polished metal of the table. When he looked up, his vision was blurred by tears, and his voice cracked as he spoke.

"I don't want to leave you alone."

His father placed a hand on Radek's shoulder. "Don't worry. I won't be alone for very long. I still intend to request a transfer back to Treya once the negotiations are done. We'll probably get Halune soon, but I'm afraid you may have ruined our chances of getting a bone drive. I'll most likely be recalled to Earth to explain why. After that, I expect they'll want to assign someone else here, whether I want to go or not."

"You mean I got you fired?"

His father smiled. "We'll see. It doesn't really matter since I was going to leave the job anyway."

"I'm sorry."

His father waved off the apology. "The goblins are demanding some sort of punishment. We're going to confine you to quarters for the next couple of days. Then, we'll let it be known that you're leaving the station." Radek started to protest, but his father lifted a hand. "One way or another you'll leave, whether it's with me or if I send you back to grandma and grandpa."

Almost involuntarily, Radek glanced at the family picture on his cabinet. Going back to Treya probably wouldn't be so bad. He turned back to his father. "What's going to happen to Ovian?"

His father's wrist chimed. He glanced down at it and sighed but didn't accept the communication.

"He'll be confined to quarters as well, though he'll be under guard. Apparently, he has a knack for sneaking out of situations like this." His father laughed and shook his head. "I suppose I shouldn't be surprised that he's been in situations like this. The goblins want something harsher, but they aren't really in a position to do anything, not since all the laws you broke were elven." His wrist chimed again. "I have to get back to these talks. You should know your door is being watched and alarm crystals have been placed in the access shafts in the ceiling."

"I thought you said only Ovian was going to be under guard."

"Ovian has guards in his room with him. I doubt that's necessary for you. Is it?" Radek shook his head and tried not to look ashamed. "I'll be back before you go to bed."

The next several hours passed in agonizing slowness. His viewscreen gave him access to dozens of entertainment programs, but elven entertainment mostly had to do with learning history, and Radek soon got tired of it. He ended up lying on his bed and staring at the ceiling, trying to trace the curved patterns the elves put on all of their structures. He wasn't sure how long he lay there before his door chimed.

"Come in," he said without moving.

The door slid open and footsteps entered the room. When no one spoke, he looked up. Ovian and the Veelan stood just inside his door. Their faces were serious, and Ovian took a step toward him.

"I'm not supposed to go with you." Radek's voice cracked as his eyes wandered to Ovian's father. This obviously wasn't a normal visit. "Aren't you supposed to be locked in your room?"

Ovian looked to his father. Tears welled in his eyes. He tried to speak, but it came out as a whimper. The Veelan put a hand on Ovian's shoulder, and he looked at Radek with a sad expression. Radek's heart skipped a beat.

"Where is my father?"

"I'm sorry, Radek. He was found in a nearby hall. His throat had been slit. He's dead."

CHAPTER 7

For a moment, Radek just stared at the elves. They had to be wrong. He'd spoken to his father only a few hours ago. How long had that been? He looked at his clock and it took him a little while to translate the elven numbers to their human counterparts. Stupid. He'd learned to do that long ago. It wasn't like it was hard. It was almost time for dinner. His father should be returning any minute. He would probably be mad if he found Ovian here, but no, that didn't make sense. Since the Veelan was here too, it would probably be fine. In fact, his father would most likely invite them for dinner. As soon as he got back, they would get it ready. The look on the Veelan's face brought him back to reality.

"Dead? How?"

The voice was so quiet that, for a moment, Radek didn't recognize it as his own. The Veelan shook his head.

"We don't know any details yet. He seemed to be on his way back here when he was attacked. The healers are examining his body to see what they can determine and security is going over the videos."

"What am I going to do now?" He was on the verge of tears.

"You're going to come live with us!" Ovian said in his usual energetic voice.

The Veelan cleared his throat, and Ovian looked away. Radek met the Veelan's eyes. The elf gave him a slow nod.

"I've sent a message to Treya. Your father sometimes spoke of family there."

Radek nodded and glanced at the picture on his dresser. "My grandma and grandpa."

"We'll see if they want to come get you, or if I'm to send you to Treya. In the meantime, you'll stay with us."

"What about the goblins? I thought they wanted me to stay in my room."

As soon as he said it, he realized it was ridiculous. What did it matter what the goblins wanted now that his father was gone?

The Veelan snorted, which seemed very unelflike to Radek. "If the Krom doesn't like it, he can take it up with me. I'll not confine a child who is guilty of nothing more than thinking like a child, not when he just lost his father." His wrist chimed, but he slid his finger over the display, rejecting the communication. "Would you like help in gathering your things or do you want me to send someone back for them?"

"My things?"

Radek looked around, but the room was blurry, and it took him a few seconds to realize there were tears in his eyes. He wiped them away, and examined his room, but he couldn't think of what he should take. Finally, his eyes locked on the holo of his family, and the room blurred again. He rubbed at his eyes and went to pick up the palm-sized projector. He waved his hand through the image. It winked out of existence, and he slipped the device into his pocket. He looked at the Veelan.

"Can I come back for the rest later?"

Why was his voice so quiet? His father had taught him to speak clearly, especially when addressing someone as important as the Veelan. Otherwise, he might be insulted. The elven leader, however, simply inclined his head.

"Of course. This is still the human enclave, and I'll give orders that no one is to come in here until you're done."

Radek's lower lip quivered. He looked over the room one last time. He couldn't think of what else to do, so he just stared at the Veelan until the elf stepped out of the room. Radek and Ovian followed right behind him. A dim part of his mind realized he was walking slowly, but neither Ovian nor his father said anything about it. He walked in a half daze, with nothing seeming real. The illusion of the forest felt subdued, and the colors less vibrant. Even the gleam of the metallic portions seemed to have lost their luster.

After walking through more corridors than Radek cared to count, they reached a large double door with flowing images carved onto it. Like many of the doors in the elven parts of the station, it looked like wood, though that was only an illusion. A pair of elves carrying crystal pikes stiffened as they approached, but they relaxed when the Veelan waved them off. The door slid open and the smells assaulted Radek.

Pine mingled with the scent of roses and honey. The ceiling was so high Radek couldn't see it. Trees with silvery blue trunks and shimmering emerald leaves reached up at least a hundred feet. Birds and insects chirped a soothing song, though Radek wasn't sure if it was a recording or the actual animals. A leaf drifted down and brushed Radek's face. It left a sappy substance on his cheek and filled his nose with a sweet scent he didn't recognize. He reached up and tried to brush it away, but his fingers came away sticky. He gaped at them before he looked up at Ovian.

"Is this real?"

Ovian looked at the canopy of braches above them. They were so intermingled Radek couldn't tell where one tree ended and the next began. "Obviously. We wouldn't want fake plants here."

"But then why do you have illusions everywhere else?"

The Veelan laughed. "It takes a great deal of resources to maintain an environment like this. Even the oxygen these plants provide isn't enough benefit. We like it though, so we do what we can. Come, I've set aside the room next to Ovian's in our tree. Even if you don't know how to climb, our song has changed the barks so stairs grew leading up to the living chambers."

"You live in trees?"

Ovian stared at him, his mouth half open. "Of course we live in trees. Where else would we live?"

The Veelan cleared his throat. "Ovian is too accustomed to the privilege of our station. Some of us live in trees. They're big enough to house multiple families each, but as I've said, it takes too many resources to maintain so many plants. There isn't enough room for all the elves, but the high ranking among us do live in trees imported from our homeworld. Who actually lives here changes as some families leave and others arrive, but it's almost always full."

"Does that mean you had to kick someone out to get me a room?"

Ovian smirked. "Yeah, but it was Fanul, though, and no one likes him."

"That's enough, Ovian. Fanul and his family are scheduled to return to Droshala next week. I convinced them to take temporary habitation in some of the ground quarters until then. They were happy to do this for you."

Radek remembered the elven boy from his classes. While none of the children had been kind, Fanul had been particularly rude, treating

Radek like he had no right to be here. "They were?"

The Veelan inclined his head. "More or less. At least, they were happy to do me a favor. I'll repay them in time, but it was the least I could do. I owe your father a great debt."

"You do?"

Ovian's father nodded. "He was a Veelan, or near enough to it, and this is my station. I was honor bound to protect him, and I failed. I will not permit harm to come to you, no matter what."

Radek looked down. "Oh."

The Veelan led them through the forest. Strange birds flitted from branch to branch above them, and the air felt heavy and thick with humidity. Even the light peeking through the branches looked more like a sun than anything artificial. For a moment, Radek could imagine he wasn't on a space station, and that his father hadn't been killed. He half expected him to come out from between the trees at any moment, but of course, he didn't.

They moved through the forest for nearly a quarter hour, following a trail only the elves seemed to see. They stopped in front of a tree that, as far as Radek could tell, looked exactly like the ones around it. Wooden stairs wound around the trunk, though enough branches and knots jutted out to make climbing possible. He'd expected to see some sort of tree house, but as far as he could tell, the branches were empty of anything but leaves.

"Where exactly do you live?"

"In cavities in the tree, of course," the Veelan said.

Radek looked up. The tree was almost impossibly tall, and its uneven bark made it hard to see any details. He suddenly started wondering if this was a good idea.

"How high?" His voice came out as a squeak.

"Yours and Ovian's rooms are about fifty feet up. Do you feel up to climbing or shall we take the stairs?"

Radek tried to spot the cavities in the tree the Veelan had spoken of, but he got dizzy before its sheer size. He suppressed a shiver. He bit is lower lip and glanced at Ovian who seemed ready to climb. His gaze lingered on the stairs for a second, not wanting to appear afraid in front of his friend. Before he could answer though, the Veelan spoke again.

"Actually, I believe I hurt my leg earlier. I think I'll take the stairs. Radek, why don't you come with me?"

Radek let out a breath of relief and nodded. Ovian spoke up. "Do I have to take the stairs too?"

The Veelan narrowed his eyes. "Yes, you do. Come now, it won't hurt you to walk a bit."

"It's just so slow."

"Ovian." The Veelan raised his voice.

"Fine, we'll take the stairs."

The thick layer of sticky sap on the stairs told Radek that they hadn't been used in a long time, and more than once, it was a struggle to get his foot unstuck. At regular intervals, they passed the cavities Ovian's father had spoken of. Some were a single room, but others were large enough to house entire families. The cavities had doors built into them, but most were open. Elves stared at them as they passed.

"They're probably laughing at us for walking," Ovian said.

"More likely, they're wondering who our guest is," the Veelan said. "He's the first human allowed into this area, after all. It's just up ahead."

The room the Veelan led him to was nothing like his room in the human enclave. The bed had been grown out of the tree itself. The mattress seemed to be wrapped in a giant leaf. There was a carpet of woven grass and crystals embedded in the wall illuminated as soon as they entered. There was a viewscreen set into a wall, as well as a cabinet with a dragon carved on each door. Radek looked at the Veelan who nodded, and Radek pulled the holo out of his pocket and placed it on top of the cabinet. He waved his hand over it, and it hummed to life, but Radek turned away before the picture appeared. He didn't want to tear up in front of the elves.

"Thank you," he said.

"I'm having dinner brought up in a few hours. Why don't you and Ovian join me?"

"But father, I was going to..." Ovian went silent when his father narrowed his eyes.

"Up until an hour ago, you thought you would still be confined to quarters for another several days. You couldn't possibly have other plans, could you?"

The tone in his voice left no doubt in Radek's mind that it wasn't really intended as a question. Ovian slumped his shoulders, and didn't meet his father's eyes.

"No, father."

"Good. I'll expect you, then." His voice softened. "Radek, what about you? I'm not familiar with the human grieving process so forgive me if I err. If you'd prefer to spend the night alone, I won't pressure you. If you'd like to come, I could arrange for some human food. I don't know how skilled my cooks are at preparing it, but they'll certainly try."

Radek bit his lower lip and glanced over his shoulder at the holo of his family. He fought back the tears and turned back to the elves.

"I'll come."

CHAPTER 8

O vian came for Radek at the appointed time. The Veelan's quarters were on the opposite side of the tree and only a little higher, so it was easier to take the stairs rather than climbing. Unlike most dwellings in the tree, this one had its door closed, though it swung inward as soon as they neared, revealing a room that was so large it had to go nearly to the center of the great tree. Ovian's mother was singing softly to a wall which seemed to be gradually changing shape. She turned when the door opened. She had golden hair that almost reached the floor, and her alabaster skin practically glowed in the light of the crystals. Her eyes were orange, a color Radek had never seen in elves. He found himself staring at them until Ovian jabbed an elbow into his side. The woman laughed, a sound that reminded Radek of bells.

"You're not the only one to be caught off guard by my eyes," she said. "It's a rare color. Some say it's an indication of dragon blood, but few of us actually believe it. Still, it does make for interesting dinner conversation." She inclined her head. "I am Mistress Malen. You have my deepest condolences for your loss."

Radek almost extended his hand to shake, but remembered at the last minute and inclined his head in return. She ushered them inside.

As soon as he had entered, he realized that he had been wrong about the size of the quarters. They weren't just big. They were immense, a veritable cavern in the tree. He could fit his entire bedroom in this chamber twice over and still have room to spare, and that was only in the part he'd seen. Two closed doors were on the wall opposite the entrance. In the middle of the room was a rectangular table of gnarled wood growing out of the ground. It was large enough to seat a dozen people, though only one chair was occupied. The Veelan sat at one end with platters of fruit and meat Radek didn't recognize on the table before him, as well as what looked like a slab of roast beef. He rose when Radek and Ovian approached and inclined his head.

"Be welcome into my home."

"Thank you," Radek said as he returned the gesture. As he looked up, he remembered that the Veelan's words were part of a greeting ceremony. He tried to remember the right response but couldn't form the thoughts. He sighed. "Sorry."

The Veelan waved off his apology. "Don't give it a second thought. How are you finding your quarters?"

"They're fine. I haven't really had time to get settled in."

"Yes, of course. Please sit." Mistress Malen sat next to him and Radek and Ovian were across from them. "Do you need anything? Your father had you in Mistress Elawn's class, but I don't think you need to continue that since you won't be staying. Of course if you enjoy it, you're free to continue, or you can join Ovian if you wish. His education is handled by a private tutor."

Mistress Malen, who was in the process of preparing a plate for Radek, stopped slicing the meat. "Dear, why don't we give him time? At least wait until you hear from his grandparents."

The Veelan looked from Malen to Radek before nodding. "Yes, of course. Forgive me. Is there anything you need?"

Radek shook his head. "No, I don't think so. Will you tell me when they call you?"

"I'll send for you as soon as I get the communication."

Radek scooped up a spoonful of orange berries into his mouth and wrinkled his nose at the sour taste. The meat was spongy and tasted a little like cherries, though Radek wasn't sure if that was the taste of the meat itself or of some spice. The silvery cup contained a watery brown liquid that tasted like pine, and Radek wondered if he was drinking elven grass. Even the roast beef had an odd minty taste to it. He smiled and said everything was delicious, but he couldn't help but wonder where his father had gotten the normal food they had eaten.

The meal itself was full of awkward conversations and long silences. The Veelan started talking about his day several times, but he'd spent most of that time with Radek's father, and he never spoke more than a few minutes before glancing at Radek and stopping. Ovian had spent the whole time under guard, and Mistress Malen had spent most of the day supervising the growing of a tree that would contain four new dwellings. That involved a lot of singing, though, and once it became apparent that all but the most basic details were beyond Radek, she too kept silent. A few minutes in, Radek found himself wishing the dinner would end, and he was thankful when the Veelan's wrist chimed.

"Excuse me," he said, rising. "It's security."

Malen nodded and the Veelan walked through one of the doors in the back of the room. Ovian pushed a piece of purple fruit around with is fork.

"Mother, can we go now?"

She sighed. "I suppose so. You'll have to forgive us, Radek. I fear this meal didn't provide as much comfort as we hoped. You will let us know if you need anything?"

Radek inclined his head. "Of course." He stumbled, trying to remember if the wife of the Veelan had a specific title. In the end, he settled for the one she'd given. "Mistress."

She smiled, and Radek had the impression he'd said something wrong but that she would never mention it. Ovian took his hand and practically dragged him out of the quarters and onto the stairs of the tree. Rather than returning to Radek's room, Ovian went up the bark next to the door. He was already ten feet up before he stopped and turned around.

"Are you coming?"

"Coming where?"

"Didn't you hear? It was security. They're probably talking about what happened to your father. We have to hurry or we'll miss it. There's the entrance to an access shaft up here."

"There are access shafts in the tree?"

"Of course. We should just be glad my mother didn't think to send guards with me. Now, come on."

Radek sighed and started climbing, though he didn't go nearly as fast as Ovian. He kept being afraid he would fall, and once, he looked down and the ground seemed impossibly far away. Finally, he reached Ovian just as the elf finished his song. The bark parted revealing a passage illuminated by green crystals. Ovian crawled in and immediately turned down a side passage. Radek came in after him. These tunnels were taller than the maintenance shafts, though not quite as wide. Still, moving through them was easier.

"You know, this is how we almost started a war yesterday," Radek said. "Didn't your father change his codes once he found out you knew them?"

"Of course he did," Ovian said without turning around, "but

those were mother's codes. They don't know I know those. Besides, we're not trying to learn state secrets this time, and it's not like we're really doing anything wrong."

"Your father is the Veelan. I'm pretty sure his conversation with security counts as state secrets."

"Well yes, but even if they find out I overheard, we're not going to go to war with ourselves. We probably won't attack you either, so there's no problem. Come on."

They didn't have far to go, and before long, Ovian stopped and started singing softly. The wall near them writhed and seemed to collapse in on itself, leaving a rounded cavity that was so thin at the bottom that Radek could see light on the other side.

"It's hard to say, Veelan," a muffled voice said from beneath them. "The weapon was definitely made on Goalton and used by someone a foot shorter than the ambassador, but whether that was elf, dwarf, or goblin, I don't know."

"What reason would an elf or dwarf have for killing Kenneth, particularly with a goblin weapon? It had to be the goblins. Krom Chernok practically delivered a threat when we refused to hand over the children."

"Perhaps someone wanted to implicate the goblins. Not everyone was happy about making peace with them. Regardless of why, something disrupted all the recorders in that hall. Bone magic could do that, but so could crystal and rune. With neither murder weapon nor witness, we can't prove anything."

"Find more, Brenar. I want whoever did this."

"By your command, Veelan."

There was a beeping sound. Ovian sang softly, and the cavity shrank, leaving no sign it had ever been there. He turned to Radek. Radek tried to speak, but the words caught in his throat. After a few tries, he managed it.

"The goblins killed my father."

"They're not really sure yet."

Radek barely heard him. He'd been caught trying to sneak into the goblin enclave. Less than half a day later, he'd been arrested for trying to steal goblin secrets. The goblins had demanded a harsh punishment, and his father and the Veelan had denied them. Within hours, they had killed his father. It was Radek's fault.

CHAPTER 9

R adek awoke to pounding on his door. He sat up and activated the lights before opening it. Ovian burst in. His face was red, and he was gasping.

"What is it?" Radek asked.

"It's the goblins," he said. "They're leaving."

Radek rolled over and put a pillow over his head. "You should be glad. At least they won't kill your father."

Ovian shook his head. "You don't understand. Every goblin in the entire station is leaving. My father gave the order to seal the station, and when the Krom demanded to know why, my father told him about the ambassador. The Krom told him to make an accusation if he could, and then he summoned soldiers. He wasn't even supposed to have soldiers on the station. That was the agreement when they lost the war. They forced their way past the guards and into their ships."

Radek sat up. "But couldn't the docking bays just keep them in?"

Ovian shook his head. "Some got out before my father gave the order, including half a dozen mid-range warships. Those turned around and targeted the station with their weapons. Father says we can defend ourselves, but it'll be a bloody contest. He sent to

Droshala for reinforcements, but he's sure the goblins have spoken to Goalton, and he doesn't know which force will get here first. He's in talks with the Krom to try to resolve this."

"Your father is with the Krom alone? They'll kill him."

Ovian shook his head. "Of course he's not with the Krom alone. Diplomatic talks with goblins have to involve at least six guards from each side, all fully armed. That's why elven guards went with your father when he met with the Krom. That's not the point, though. We can't let them get away."

Radek fell back into his bed. "I'm sure your father will stop them."

Ovian grabbed Radek's arm and tugged him to a sitting position. The elf looked genuinely scared. "That's the thing. He won't. If the goblin reinforcements get here first, they'll have enough firepower to destroy the station. He can't risk everyone just to keep the goblins here. They're going to get away. Even if he wanted to help you, the debt he owes your father is to keep you safe, not to find his killer. He'll let them go. We have to sneak on to one of the goblin ships."

For a second, Radek stared at him, unsure if the elf was serious. After a few seconds Ovian went to the cabinet and started pulling out clothes and throwing them at Radek. Radek got out of bed and grabbed Ovian by the shoulder. The elf turned around and handed Radek a shoe.

"Are you crazy?" he asked. "That's how we almost started a war last time."

"The goblins already started this war. It's not like we can do anymore harm. We can't let the ones who killed your father get away."

"How would we even get on a ship? The last time we tried didn't exactly turn out well for us."

Ovian looked at the ceiling. "We weren't trying to get on a ship last time. We were trying to get information from the golem. This is completely different. I know we'll be able to get on."

"Are you sure?"

"I'm positive, but we have to go now if we're going to make it."

"I'm sorry. I can't allow that." Radek looked up to see an elven guard standing in his doorway. He held a crystal pike in his right hand, though he kept the point away from them. He glanced at Ovian and shook his head. "Veelani Ovian, your father thought you might try something like this. He sent me to make sure you and your friend stay out of trouble."

"We weren't going to do anything," Ovian said.

The guard snorted, obviously having heard a similar claim before. Ovian looked at Radek and winked, though his head leaned heavily to one side as he did, making the gesture obvious. Radek glanced at the guard, but he seemed not to have noticed. Apparently, it was only obvious if you knew human body language, and it didn't look like this elf did.

"I need to go see my mother," Ovian said before anyone could do anything.

The guard looked at him for a second before nodding. "Very well. I'll take the two of you up there."

"No, not both of us. Just me."

The guard shook his head, and gave them a half smile. "I'm no fool, Veelani, and you've escaped from me before. I was instructed to guard you both. Your friend comes with us or we stay here. Those are the only two options."

Ovian's sighed. "Fine. Radek, do you mind coming with us? It won't be long."

Radek pursed his lips. What was Ovian up to? Finally he shrugged.

Ovian stared at him and tried to repeat the gesture, but he jerked his shoulders up so fast it almost looked like he was having a seizure. Radek suppressed a smile.

"All right, let's go."

They exited the room and started walking around the tree on the stairs. Ovian kept looking down and then back to Radek. They had only gone halfway around the tree before Radek decided that Ovian was right. They couldn't let those goblins escape, but the only option he could think of was a bad one.

"When we fell out of the access shafts, one of the elves used a song to slow our fall."

"Yes, most guards are familiar with that one."

"Does that help you protect us?" Radek asked.

The guard smiled. "It does if you fall."

"Oh. Good."

Without warning, Radek grabbed the guard's wrist in one hand and Ovian's in the other. Humans were naturally stronger than elves, and he didn't have any trouble pulling the others off their feet as he leaped off the stairs, dragging them with him.

CHAPTER 10

Though Radek had been expecting it, he screamed as they fell. The guard yelped, but started singing almost instantly. The rush of wind lessened, but the guard stumbled over his words and the ground shot up at them, knocking the breath out of Radek when he hit. Pain shot through him as he rolled onto his back. The guard groaned next to him, and Ovian grimaced as he got up.

"That was brilliant." Ovian's near constant jovial attitude had been eroded by his injuries, but the elf still showed signs of it. "Even I would've never thought of leaping off the tree." He offered Radek a hand up. "Are you all right?"

Radek winced but nodded. He glanced at the guard whose chest was rising and falling slowly in the regular rhythm of breath. The elf didn't open his eyes, though.

"I didn't mean to hurt him. I thought he'd just sing, and we'd all be fine. Then, we could run away."

Ovian looked up toward the canopy. "You surprised him." Ovian poked the guard and sang a few words. His back arched a little as Ovian finished his song. "He'll survive for a while, at least long enough for someone to find him and call the healers. He'll be fine, but we should go."

Radek nodded and Ovian ran off. In spite of his injuries, the elf wasn't slowed, and Radek struggled to keep up. Rather than going to the entrance of the enclave, Ovian led him to a rock wall. The elf extended a hand, and his fingers passed through the stone. There was a click, and Ovian started climbing, his arms and legs almost constantly disappearing beneath the illusion over the wall. He went up about ten feet before he vanished into the rock. Radek reached forward and his hands found a metal ladder. He looked around to make sure no one was watching and climbed up slowly, uneasy about not being able to see where he was putting his hands and feet. His muscles screamed in pain every time he went up a step. He thought he heard movement behind him and hurried through the hidden hole. As soon as he was in, Ovian let out a long breath before turning and crawling through the corridors. Several times, Radek thought he heard shouting from beneath them, but Ovian never slowed. They'd been crawling for nearly an hour when a screen Radek hadn't realized was there came to life on the wall. The Veelan's face appeared.

"Ovian, Radek, I know you're there. The sensors have detected you. Please respond."

Ovian crawled by it without pausing, but he stopped when Radek did.

"Shouldn't we answer?" Radek asked.

"He's just going to want us to go back, and we're not going to do that anyway, so there's no point."

"Please," the Veelan said. "You're heading in the direction of a docking bay that holds a dozen goblin ships. If they catch you, they'll kill you."

"Good," Ovian said as he started crawling again.

"How can that be good?" Radek asked.

"I wasn't actually sure we were heading in the right direction.

Now, I know."

For a second, Radek just stared. Then, he hurried to follow. A bruise on his left knee sent pangs of pain shooting up his leg, but he forced himself to ignore it. Another screen came to life ahead of them. Once again, the Veelan's image asked them to respond, but they ignored this one as well.

"We can't exit before we get into the docking bay like we did last time," Ovian said. "The door will be guarded. We'll have to go to one of the larger docking bays that have floor access to the shafts. I'm pretty sure that one has goblin ships in it too."

"Stay where you are," the Veelan said from the screen. "I'm sending soldiers into the access shafts to get you. Someone should be there in a few minutes."

Ovian turned down a corridor, and the ceiling gradually lowered until it was barely two feet from the ground. Radek practically had to drag himself forward on his stomach.

"Oh no." The Veelan's eyes went wide. "You're actually trying to get on a goblin ship aren't you? Ovian, I don't know what you said to Radek to convince him to do this, but please stop. Radek, my debt to your father. I must pay it."

Ovian stiffened for a second before continuing. The Veelan turned to someone.

"Give clearance for the goblin ships to leave."

"Sir?" someone said off screen.

"Do it now. I want them off the station as quickly as possible. Within two minutes. Faster."

Radek had never seen such a look of terror on the face of an elf before. "Why would he do that?"

"I didn't expect that," Ovian said. "If all the ships are gone, we can't get into one. We need to hurry."

Radek pushed himself forward as fast as he could. He clenched his teeth against the pain the movement brought on. Suddenly the ceiling began to vibrate. A few seconds later, the entire corridor was shaking.

"What's happening?"

"A ship is taking off. I'm not sure how many are in this docking bay, but they can't take off all at once. As long as there's at least three, we should have time to get on one, or at least we will if we hurry."

"I'm going as fast as I can."

"Go faster!"

Abruptly, the vibration lessened to a gentle shaking, and the blood drained from Radek's face as he envisioned his father's killers getting away.

"Are we too late?"

"I don't think so. There must've been a ship right above us. This will have to be good enough."

He started singing, and a hatch appeared in the corridor ceiling. The rumbling became a roar as heat and sound poured in. Ovian stood up and climbed out. Radek stood, though he couldn't pull himself out until Ovian offered him a hand up, and he climbed into the docking bay.

There was only one ship left, a massive vessel in the shape of a large bird with weapons practically covering the wings. It had three landing struts, but they were already being raised. Ovian grabbed Radek's wrist, and they started running for the nearest one. The roar of the ship's engines was deafening, and Radek thought his head would explode, but he ran on. He leaped, and his hand closed around a metal support. He was lifted up as the landing strut was drawn into the ship. Ovian latched on to his leg, barely avoiding the hatch that closed beneath him, sealing them inside of the goblin ship.

CHAPTER 11

"How much do you know about these ships?" Radek asked.

Ovian started singing, and a crystal in his hand glowed, casting odd shadows on the elf's face. They were in a sort of undercarriage. Cables hung from the ceiling which was only about five feet off the ground. There didn't seem to be a way out other than the way they had come in.

"A little. I think this is a goblin fell flyer. What do you want to know?"

The ship groaned as it started moving.

"If we'll be able to breathe in this part of the ship once we go into space."

"Oh, that's a good point. Hold on." Ovian took a pair of crystals out of a pouch at his belt and sang. They flickered for a second, and he passed one to Radek. "That'll hold the air around you and purify it so you can keep breathing it. As long as I recharge them every couple of hours, we'll be fine. "

Radek stared at his friend for several seconds before letting out a long breath. He looked strange in the dim light. "Ovian, what are we doing here?"

"What do you mean? We're here to make sure the one who killed your father doesn't get away."

"Yes, but we don't even know who that is. I mean think about it. How many ships did the goblins have at the station?"

"I don't know. Fifty or so."

"And the killer could be on any one of them."

"But they're all going to the same place." He didn't sound very sure of himself. "They probably are." Ovian's sighed. "I guess we really didn't think this all the way through. What do we do now?"

Before Radek could answer, the ship hummed and started to shake. There was a roar, and they were thrown against the back wall, reawakening all of Radek's wounds. Almost instantly, heat leeched out of the undercarriage. Radek's breath misted, and his teeth chattered. He could still breathe, but the air was so cold it burned his lungs. Ovian was pressed against the wall a few feet away from him. He seemed to be trying to say something, but Radek didn't hear a sound from his direction. The pressure holding him against the wall increased until he thought it would crush him. His eyes started to bulge as the air was pressed out of his lungs. Pain ran up his arm as Ovian's crystal was pressed into his hand by the force holding him to the wall. Stars swam in his vision, and the world began to grow dark.

Suddenly, Ovian pushed a second crystal into Radek's hand, and air rushed into him. The cold didn't vanish entirely, but it receded to that of a mild winter day. He collapsed onto his hands and knees, breathing heavily. It was a few minutes before he was even able to attempt speech again.

"What...What happened?"

A faint mist surrounded Ovian and he cupped his hand to his ear. Radek repeated the question. Ovian shook his head and tapped his ear. His brow wrinkled in confusion, but that melted away as his eyes widened and a smile appeared on his face. He took a few steps toward Radek until the mist surrounding him joined with a similar bubble around Radek.

"Sorry, I forgot. Sound needs air to travel through, and there isn't any here apart from my charm." He glanced down. "Oh, we should take care of that hand."

Radek followed the elf's gaze. The crystal Ovian had given him for breathing had been partially pressed into his hand, and blood drizzled out. Ovian pulled out another crystal and sang for a second before handing it to Radek.

"You can keep that one in your pocket. It should heal your wounds by morning."

Radek nodded and put the crystal in his pocket. The room stopped spinning a little, and words came easier. "What happened?"

Ovian looked at the ceiling. "The ship left the station. I knew we needed breath charms, but the rest of it caught me off guard. I didn't realize space was so cold, and I never even thought about doing a motion charm."

Radek blinked. The world still seemed to be spinning. "A motion charm?"

Ovian nodded. "The ship accelerates very quickly. Without a motion charm, that would crush us."

"I think it almost did."

"Yeah, sorry about that. Ships have permanent charms in place to handle all that in the inhabited areas. It's easy to forget they're there."

Radek rubbed the back of his head and winced when he touched a bump. "Try not to forget about those next time. Can we get into one of the safe areas of the ship? We don't know how long we'll be here, and it would probably be better to be in one of those permanent charm areas."

Ovian huffed. "I won't forget." He looked at the ceiling. "You're probably right, though. I could've maintained two charms on each of us for days, but I don't think I could do three for very long."

Ovian helped Radek up, though the pain of his wounds seemed to have subsided. Ovian could walk upright without any problem, though Radek had to stoop to avoid pieces of metal jutting down from the ceiling. They walked around the length of the undercarriage but didn't see a way to access the inhabited areas of the ship. Almost everything was cold to the touch. It was only in a small nook near the back that the air started to warm. There was a gentle hum as well as the faint echo of screaming that sent chills down Radek's spine. Ovian's eyes went wide.

"I think we're near the bone drive."

Radek looked up and laid his hand on the metal ceiling. It felt soft, as if it was covered in carpet, and as soon as he touched it, a jolt of energy ran up his arm. He pressed harder, but the metal wouldn't give.

"Can you use your heat charm on this? It already feels a little soft. Maybe we can melt our way through."

Ovian reached up, but he wasn't tall enough so Radek had to give him a boost. The elf closed his eyes, but after a few seconds, he shook his head.

"It's heated by goblin magic. If I were to use my charm, it would be a different kind of heat, and they wouldn't combine."

"But it's just heat," Radek said as he put his friend down. "How can heat be different?"

Ovian looked at the ceiling. "I don't know. It just is."

Radek reached up with the second crystal Ovian had given him and held it against the ceiling. Again, he felt that strange energy, and he twitched as the crystal shocked him. He stared at it, but didn't see anything different so he pressed it harder. Without knowing exactly how he did it, he pulled at something. The ceiling sizzled, and the faint smell of burning sulfur filled Radek's air bubble. He withdrew the crystal, and revealed a tiny hole in the metal. It hissed as air rushed into the compartment. Ovian gaped at it.

"I'm pretty sure that's impossible."

He took the crystal from Radek's hand and looked into it. Instantly, a wave of cold washed over Radek, and he was thrown against the back wall. He cried out as the momentum began crushing him into the metal. Ovian gasped and ran over to him and pressed the crystal into Radek's hand.

"Sorry. I wasn't thinking."

Radek groaned. "Can you please stop almost killing me?"

"You act like I've done it more than once."

"You've done it twice."

Ovian's eyes darted around. "You mean when the ship first took off? That time almost killed me too. I don't think that one should count."

Radek narrowed his eyes. "If it almost killed me, it counts."

Ovian let out a breath. "Fine. I'm sorry for almost killing you twice."

"Why did you take the crystal from me anyway?"

Ovian glanced at the melted hole. "I wanted to see if it had gotten stronger. There's no way what I did to it could've melted that metal."

"Well, is it stronger?"

Ovian shook his head. "It doesn't make sense. Maybe if I could see the bone drive..."

Radek pursed his lips. "But can you make my crystal stronger?"

Ovian looked at the ceiling. "Maybe a little, but I'm trying to preserve my energy. Why?"

"So I can use it to melt all the way through."

"I told you that won't work."

"You also told me the crystal wouldn't melt through it at all."

"It shouldn't have."

Radek sighed. "Do you have any better ideas?" He lifted a crystal. "I'd really rather not die when the magic in these runs out."

Ovian's eyes darted around. "I said I was sorry."

"You can make up for it by making my crystal stronger."

Ovian held up his own crystal and sang a few words. It flickered and he held it out to Radek. "Let's trade. It's easier that way. Don't let go of yours until you're touching mine. I hope this works. Otherwise, I just wasted magic that could be used keeping us alive."

Radek nodded. Briefly, he considered snatching Ovian's crystal out of his hand so the elf would know what it felt like to be crushed against the wall, but he dismissed the idea as needlessly cruel. They exchanged crystals, and Radek felt like he was out on a spring day. He limped over to the spot he'd been in before, wincing whenever he put weight on his left leg. He glared at Ovian, but the elf just stared back. Radek sighed and put the crystal to the metal. Again, there was that peculiar shocking sensation followed by an impulse to pull, and after a few seconds, the crystal sank in, the metal around it turning cherry red. Radek dragged it in a slow circle, being careful to avoid the molten drops of metal that hissed as they hit the ground. After a minute, he completed the circle and a piece of metal clattered to the floor. Its edges quickly went from glowing orange to dull grey. A gentle green light poured in from above. They waited for a few seconds for the hole to cool before pulling themselves up into the chamber of the goblin bone drive.

CHAPTER 12

Radek wasn't sure what kind of skull it was, but whatever creature it had come from could've almost swallowed him whole. It was half as tall as he himself was, with an extended jaw and teeth as long as his fingers. A green light pulsed within, with beams periodically shining out from the eyes and illuminating spots along one of the walls. Strangely enough, every time the eyes lit up, they shone on a different spot. The hum of the engines came from behind the wall. It reminded Radek of people screaming. For a second, he could only stare.

According to the science of every race, travelling faster than the speed of light was impossible. The only way to achieve the speed that made interstellar travel feasible was to use something that wasn't confined by the rules of science. It was why it had taken humans so much longer to leave Earth than the other races. While humans had turned away from magic and embraced science, the others had used magic to do what science could never do alone. The only way to travel among the stars was to blend the two powers. Every spacefaring race had created a star drive that functioned on their own unique magic, and the working of such a drive was often one of their most closely guarded secrets.

The room itself was shaped like a dome of silvery red metal. The curved wall distorted their reflections and made it look like they each wore a wicked grin. The goblin drive stood on a pile of bleached bones, and it almost seemed to be looking at him as it powered the engines. Radek stepped to one side, and a light followed him. He couldn't help but meet its gaze, and his blood went cold. He told himself he was imagining things, but he couldn't quite convince himself.

"We should get out of here," he said as he glanced at the hole he'd made. He didn't understand why the floor was red while the piece of metal he'd cut had been gray, but there wasn't really time to figure that out. "They probably detected that. They'll be on their way."

"Good idea," Ovian said.

"Which way do we go?"

Ovian looked up at the curved ceiling. "Why do you think I know?"

"You said you know a little about these ships. That's more than I know."

"Oh, well...I don't actually know anything about the inside. I built models of most of the goblin ships, but those just dealt with the outside."

Radek rolled his eyes. There was a door at one end of the room and Radek headed in that direction. It slid open as they approached, and Ovian drew back. The passageway was made of black metal. Red lights pulsed in the ceiling.

"What is that sound?" Ovian's voice was practically a shout.

"What sound?"

Ovian covered his ears and continued to speak loudly. "Can't you hear it? It's making my head hurt. It sounds like an alarm."

A memory from Mistress Elawn's class drifted to the surface of his mind. Goblins had a hearing range that extended into a higher frequency than humans. There were even records of dog whistles causing them pain. Elves, if he remembered correctly, could also hear higher than humans.

"It probably is an alarm," Radek said. "We need to find a place to hide."

They rushed down the hall until they reached a wall with passages heading in opposite directions. Radek looked from one to the other, but Ovian dashed down the hall to the left.

"Do you know where you're going?" Radek asked as he followed.

"I already told you I don't. If we don't know where to go anyway, we might as well just pick one at random."

A slit opened in the wall ahead of them, and as they ran by it a gout of flame exploded toward them. Ovian cried out, and Radek fell to the ground, the fire searing the air above him. He crawled forward and found Ovian on the other side of the trap. The back part of his robes were singed, but he seemed otherwise unharmed.

"That was...look out!"

Radek turned and the flame expanded, filling the hall. He got to his feet, and they ran. Guns lowered out of the ceiling and fired a steady stream of glowing balls of energy. Ovian grabbed his hand, and they darted from one side of the hall to another. More than once, one of the balls hit Radek, filling his nostrils with the scent of burning flesh.

They rounded a corner and found a hall lined with metal doors. Sentry guns spaced every several feet pointed at them, but before they started firing, Ovian pulled Radek through one of the doors and into a long room filled with iron crates. They took several deep breaths, and the pain that Radek hadn't noticed blossomed to life. He clenched his teeth and tried to resist crying out. He examined his arms and found several blackened spots.

"Goblin internal defenses," Ovian said. "I told you they were strong."

"Can you do anything about these burns?"

Ovian shook his head. "The crystal I gave you will help you heal faster, but I can't do anything more than that. Healing is specialized magic. Even most full singers don't know much more than the basics."

Radek tried to get up, but pain shot through his leg, and he looked down and saw a cluster of three burns on his left knee. He hadn't even noticed when he'd been hit there. Ovian had been hit a few times too, but his injuries weren't nearly as bad. He walked over to Radek and looked him up and down. Without saying a word, he tore a strip off his robes and wrapped it around the wounded knee.

"I don't think there are defenses in here," Ovian said. "It looks like it's a storage room. Maybe there's something here we can use."

Radek tried to get up, but again, the pain kept him from rising, and he fell back to the ground. He leaned against a crate and shook his head.

"You'll have to find it, then. I can't even stand up."

Ovian opened a box and peered in but shook his head. He looked in three more before he pulled out a pipe about four feet long and handed it to Radek. By leaning his weight against it, he was able to stand.

"How long do you think it'll be before the goblins find us?"

Ovian looked around before glancing at the ceiling. "I'm not sure. They have to know someone is on board from that hole you made, but I don't think goblins have good ship-wide sensors. They'll have to look for us the slow way."

"Maybe we'll get lucky and they won't find us."

"Maybe," Ovian said, though he sounded as unsure as Radek felt.

They kept searching through the crates. For the most part, they just found spare parts. One crate contained a panel like the ones that made up the floor, including the floor of the engine room.

Radek's blood went cold. "Hide. Now."

"Why?"

"I cut a hole in the floor, and this is probably the closest place parts are stored."

Understanding dawned on Ovian and he climbed into a crate. There was a series of clanks before it went silent. Radek didn't think he'd be able to manage the same, so he limped to the back of the room and hid in a small space behind a box. They waited for what felt like hours. Radek's legs began to cramp. After a while, the crystals in his pocket heated for a second and went cold. He grabbed one, but he couldn't tell what had happened.

The door slid open and Radek went still. He smelled the goblin before he heard it, a strong leathery smell that made his heart beat faster. He found himself looking for a place to run before forcing himself to calm down. In his mind, he recited the facts. This was perfectly natural. When goblins were angry, they gave off a fear pheromone that affected most sentient races. Radek had just never experienced it, and he'd never expected the emotion to be so intense. His heart was racing. He took deep breaths, but he froze, worried that he'd been breathing too loudly. The goblin didn't seem to notice, though. Heavy footsteps came into the room and there was the sound of one of the crates being opened. The goblin grunted and started walking out. Radek let out a sigh of relief when there was a clanking sound. The goblin stopped. He grunted something in his own language. A few seconds later, he called again. Footsteps came back into the room. Keeping his head near the ground, Radek peeked around the corner of his box.

The goblin was as tall as Radek himself. He, at least Radek thought it was male, wore some sort of robot suit with indicators lighting up on his wrists. Only his head was exposed, showing a green hairless scalp. He was pushing off the lid of the box Ovian had hidden in. Radek didn't think. He pushed through the pain and launched himself at the goblin, swinging his pipe at the unprotected head. It rang like a bell, and the impact ran up Radek's arm. The goblin collapsed in a motionless heap, and Radek had to lean against a box to remain standing. His pipe was bent on the spot he'd hit with.

Ovian climbed out and looked from Radek to the goblin. He poked at the top of the goblin's head before smiling.

"He's going to be out for a while."

Radek let out a breath he hadn't realized he was holding. "He's not dead?"

Ovian shook his head. "A goblin's skull is only a little softer than steel. We should still get out of here before he wakes up. First though..."

He knelt and rolled the goblin onto his back. The metal suit made him look twice as big as he actually was. There was a star pin affixed to its chest, and Ovian worked it free before depositing it in his pocket.

"What was that?"

"I told you. Goblin sensors aren't that great. They can't really tell one life form from another. The internal defenses know not to fire on anyone that has this pin. Now we can walk around without worrying about that."

"Shouldn't I have one too?"

Ovian looked at the ceiling. "There was only one. Don't worry.

I'm pretty sure you'll be fine as long as we stay close together."

"You're pretty sure?" Ovian nodded. "Maybe I should be the one to hold it."

"I'm the one that picked it up."

"Off a goblin that I knocked out, who was coming after you because you didn't know how to keep quiet."

"I know how to keep quiet. I just slipped."

"You just promised to stop almost getting me killed."

"You'll be fine. Besides, we don't really have time to argue about this. Just grab another pipe, and follow me."

Radek grumbled but picked a new one out of the crate Ovian had been hiding in. He walked to the doorway and took Ovian's arm. They both held their breaths as they stepped out. The guns still hung from the ceiling. They twitched but otherwise remained still. As Radek and Ovian hobbled down the hall, Radek kept his eye on the weapons, half expecting them to fire. They picked a door at random and rushed through before anyone came into the hall.

This room seemed to be an empty crew quarter. There was a single bed, and Radek pressed down on it. The mattress didn't seem to be much softer that the metal forming the ship. A window looked out on what looked to be a gaseous cloud shifting from blue to purple and back again. Radek found himself drawn in by the changing colors. They swirled and he could almost make out shapes in the cloud. It was only when Ovian cleared his throat that Radek blinked and looked away. Hyperspace had a hypnotic effect on those who weren't trained to resist it. Normally, it was harmless, but when hiding on an enemy ship the distraction could kill him. Ovian helped him to the bed, but he didn't dare lie down. The elf searched the room, but found nothing and eventually sat next to Radek.

"What do we do now?" Radek asked.

Ovian looked over Radek's wounds. "I didn't think it would be like this." He buried his face in his hands. "I don't know."

"Maybe once we tear out of hyperspace, we can find a way back to *Vanel.*"

"Maybe, but who knows how long that will be? We could be travelling for days. What are we going to do about food and water?"

Radek blinked. "I never even thought of that. There have to be other storage rooms. One of them will have food."

"Assuming we don't get caught, you mean."

Radek nodded. His friend's sudden change in attitude really bothered Radek, but he could think of nothing to do about that. "Yes, assuming that. Do you have a better idea?"

Ovian shook his head. Suddenly, the ship lurched. There was a ripping sound and the cloud outside vanished, replaced by the darkness of space. Ovian and Radek exchanged glances.

"Are we there?" Radek asked.

Ovian shook his head. "We can't be. Goblin ships don't go that fast, and we weren't in hyperspace long enough to get into their territory. We might have passed the human border, but I really don't think the goblins were going there. Maybe it's not on purpose. You could've damaged the bone drive when we came in."

Ovian hopped off the bed and walked to the window. He peered around before looking over his shoulder. "We're orbiting a gas giant, but I can't see the star. The other goblin ships are here too." He looked back and gasped. "There's a space station. I didn't see it until they put it between us and the planet. It's made of the same black metal as their ships. The goblins built a space station in elven territory."

CHAPTER 13

W e have to get word to my father," Ovian said.

"Sure," Radek said. "Do you have any idea how to do that?"

"I don't know. We find a communication terminal on the station. I know the codes to the elven diplomatic channels."

"Aren't those supposed to be secret?" Ovian stared at him, and Radek let out a breath. "Never mind. I forgot who I was talking to. I don't think we need to leave though. They probably have communications somewhere on the ship."

"That's a good idea. We won't have to risk going out into the station. Maybe if we can get in contact with *Vanel*, someone can tell us how to steal this ship and get back there." He examined the walls and his eyes locked onto an air vent. "We should get in there. When they find that goblin you knocked out, they'll come looking for us."

Radek nodded, and Ovian went to work on the vent. He used Radek's pipe, though without any real tools, it took several minutes for him to pry it open. Radek winced. Anyone who saw it would immediately know it had been forced open, but there was nothing to do about that. The window revealed they had docked in the station. That had been too quick, and it would make escaping that much harder. They exchanged glances before crawling into the vent. Radek resisted the urge to groan every time he put weight on his knee, though the pain had lessened thanks to Ovian's healing crystal.

Unlike the access shafts in *Vanel*, these hadn't been built for people to walk through and were consequently much smaller. The sides scraped Radek's shoulders as he crawled through. Ovian's thinner frame had an easier time of it, but even he was cramped. The vent tilted up at times and when they came to a fork, Ovian picked a direction without hesitation.

"I thought you didn't know anything about the inside of these ships." Radek said after Ovian made the fifth such decision.

"I don't."

"Then, how do you know where we're going?"

"I'm guessing."

"You're guessing?"

"Do you have a better idea?"

"Just because I don't have a better idea doesn't mean that this is a good one."

"Better a bad one than no one."

"No, I don't think that's the case."

"Come on. It's this way."

"You don't know that."

"Fine, let's go the other way."

"That's not what I mean."

Ovian stopped and glanced over his shoulder. The motion caused a cloud of dust to fall from the ceiling of the vent. Ovian coughed for a second as the dust settled. Then, he glared at Radek.

"Look, we don't know what to do or where to go. If you just want to stay in one place and wait for the goblins to find you, fine, do that, but there's only one reason the goblins would build a station here."

All signs of childishness were gone from Ovian's face. "I'm not sure where I'm going, but I do know that what I need isn't here. You can follow me or not, but stop complaining about it."

Radek stopped as Ovian continued to crawl away. He realized how foolish he was being. He was trapped in a goblin ship in an illegal space station. If he was caught, it wouldn't be like those times on *Vanel*. There was no elven noble to get them out of trouble. The goblins would just kill them. Ovian was right. They had to do something.

He crawled after his friend, catching up a minute later. The elf was staring out of a vent. Radek tried to look out, but there wasn't enough room.

"I think this is it." Ovian said. "I see computer terminals."

He reached forward to try to push open the vent, but Radek grabbed his wrist. Ovian glared at him.

"What are you doing? I thought you decided not to do nothing."

"I did," Radek said, "but we only just landed, and they're searching for us. Don't you think we should wait a little while until we're sure everyone is off the ship?"

Ovian pulled back, and his faced softened. "Oh. Yeah, that's probably a good idea."

They waited for several minutes before Radek broke the silence. "If they really built this station to attack the elves, they must've known they were going to threaten *Vanel*."

Ovian nodded. "I know. We have to tell *Vanel*."

Radek hesitated. "But if you tell the elves that this is here, won't they destroy it?"

"Probably."

"Do you think they'll get us out first?"

"I hope so."

"But you're not sure?"

Ovian shook his head. "I joke around a lot, but I'm a Veelani, and I've spent all my life learning what that means. My duty is to the elven people. I don't think the station is heavily guarded right now, but that can't last. If the goblins are allowed to bring in reinforcements, it could give them a huge advantage in the war. I'm sorry I dragged you into this, Radek, but I have to stop that if I can."

Radek thought for a second before nodding. He didn't want to be on the space station if the elves blew it up, but the goblins had already killed his father and started a war against the human's greatest allies. If they won, what would that mean for the human race, which was just starting to establish itself among the stars?

They waited in silence for several minutes. A few times, the sounds of goblins moving through the ship drifted to them, but no one entered the room they were looking into. Finally, the silence of the ship stretched on. Ovian looked at Radek who nodded, and together, they pushed open the vent and crawled into the room.

CHAPTER 14

The room had monitors all over the walls, each with its own control panel. Lights and switches were labeled with goblin words Radek didn't know. Ovian pushed passed him and tapped a screen which came to life. He started tapping images seemingly at random.

"You read Goblin?" Radek asked.

Ovian looked at the ceiling. "A little. My father always got onto me about learning the languages of the major races. I can understand it spoken all right, but I never got the hang of reading it."

He swiped across the screen and tapped an image. Jagged characters flowed across the monitor. Ovian tapped the screen several times, entering into different parts of the system. After a few minutes, he lifted his arms in frustration. Radek moved in next to him.

"Wait," he said. "Go back."

"Go back to where?"

Radek pushed him aside and returned to the previous screen. He tapped a word, and it expanded into a list of files. He ran his fingers down the list, only struggling over the names a little. They weren't all individual files though. Some were groupings of related files, and when he would tap those, they expanded.

"You understand Goblin?"

"My father made me study the major languages before I came to *Vanel*." Radek grinned. "It's almost as bad a written language as Elven."

"Elven isn't a bad written language."

Radek shrugged. After a second, he smiled and looked up at the ceiling in an exaggerated gesture. "I guess I can understand why you would think that, if it's the only written language you know."

Ovian let out a breath. "If you're a stupid human..."

"This terminal doesn't have communications access," he said. He let out a low whistle. "Or security. I have full access to all their files. It's like they don't care about keeping any secrets."

"They tend to focus more on offense than defense," Ovian said, "and I think we're in a secure area. If they catch anyone looking at something they shouldn't, they just kill them." Radek pulled back, but Ovian laughed. "You might as well keep going. It's not like they're going to kill us any less if we stop now."

Radek scowled at him before nodding and continuing scrolling through the files. One group had a timestamp less than a day old. Radek opened the file list, and Ovian's eyes went wide.

"That's Elven."

Radek nodded and scrolled through the files, he opened one up at random, and a group of stars appeared on the screen. Numbers and letters indicating gravitational tides and eddies and radiation levels appeared, with lines connecting the values to different letters.

"It looks like a star map." Ovian traced some of the lines. "These are hyperspace routes, I think."

Radek closed the file and opened another. This one appeared to be a ship's log, but Radek didn't see anything remarkable in it. A third was another star map, and a fourth was a collection of elven legends.

"It looks like they stole this," Ovian said, "but why? There's nothing here my father wouldn't have given them if they asked."

"This word," Radek indicated a file grouping. "I think it means secret or confidential."

He tapped it, and another list of files appeared on the screen. He opened one, and the screen displayed symbols he didn't recognize, though they were definitely elven.

"Those look like magical formulae," Ovian said running his finger over one line. "It's not crystal magic. This symbol," he held his hand over an arc with star symbol superimposed on it. "I know I've seen it before. It's some sort of metal based magic."

"Gold?"

Ovian nodded. "Yes, that's it."

"Dragons use gold in their magic."

"There are no dragons anymore," Ovian said by rote. "They left known space a long time ago."

"But their magic is still around. The dwarves use it all the time. Maybe the goblins found a dragon artifact. They had a bunch of routes marked on the star charts. Maybe they found a star drive."

Ovian shuddered. "Let's hope not. Dragon drives were the fastest there ever was. We've been trying to understand how they work for centuries, but we never had a working drive to study." He scanned over the file for a few seconds. "This is our research. If the goblins find one, we can't let them figure out how to use it. Can you delete the files?"

"I think so, but what if they've made a copy of it?"

"What if they haven't?"

"Good point." Radek typed in a few commands and the list of files vanished. "There, I think that's it."

"You think?"

Radek rolled his eyes. "Now you know how it feels. Look, I just don't know if there are backups. It's as much as I can do. I might be able to find a map of the ship." He navigated through the system for a few minutes before a two-dimensional representation of the ship appeared. One room near the back was blinking, and he guessed that's where they were. He tapped several of the rooms nearby until he found the one he was looking for. "There's a communication room just down the hall." He glanced toward the vent and shook his head. "It's not in the direction those go in. We'll have to take the hall."

"Is there anyone else on the ship?"

Radek tapped the control panel. "I can't tell. I don't think so. This is hard to understand."

"I thought you could read Goblin."

"I can understand it a little, but this is all so technical."

Ovian stared at the screen for a few seconds before nodding. "All right. Let's go."

CHAPTER 15

Their footsteps echoed down the empty hall. Everything smelled of old leather, and many of the metal plates lining the wall were dented. The guns hanging from the ceiling occasionally twitched in their direction as they passed, and Radek made sure to stay close to Ovian. The door to the communication room slid open as he pressed a panel next to it, and they stepped inside. A large viewscreen made up most of one wall, and a control panel sat in front of it. They stared at it for a few seconds before Radek realized Ovian was waiting for him to activate it. He walked up to it, but hesitated.

"You realized they'll probably be able to detect it if we send a message."

Ovian nodded once. "I know."

Radek nodded and pressed buttons on the control panel. After a few tries, he managed to find the correct sequence to activate it. As before, there were no security measures on the system, and it only took him a few minutes to navigate through the system and configure it to send a message. He turned to Ovian.

"Enter the diplomatic channel codes." Ovian walked over and stared at the control panel for a few seconds. He looked down at his fingers and wrinkled his brow at the unfamiliar characters. Radek cleared his throat. "The numbers are on the top row."

Ovian glared at him but nodded. He entered the channel and security code, but the screen flashed red. Radek gasped and looked to the door, but no one came in. He turned back to the screen and read the words before letting out a breath of relief. It was just an error message. He told Ovian, who had scrambled behind a console. The elf tried again, but got the same result.

"Did you remember to translate it?"

"What do you mean translate? It's all numbers."

"Goblins have a base twelve numbering system." Ovian gave him a blank look. "They have six fingers on each hand."

"I know that."

Radek rolled his eyes and sighed. He ran his fingers over the numbers. "They have digits for zero through eleven, not just zero through nine like we do." He held two fingers over the last two number keys on the control panel, numbers that Ovian hadn't touched when he'd entered the codes. "These are ten and eleven. The channel is a frequency, right?"

"Yes."

"You have to translate."

"How do I do that?"

"I thought you had a private tutor."

"Well yes, but he taught me about magic, not about numbers."

Radek thought for a second and realized that all of his own education in math and science had come before he'd reached *Vanel*. As a diplomat's son in a time when human interstellar travel was still relatively new, his father had thought it important that he be at least familiar with the basic concepts of the mathematics of different races. The elven school, on the other hand, had focused on culture and the magic of various races, never touching on the more technical aspects. Radek did a quick search of the communication system, but didn't find any sort of calculation program so he did it by hand. He entered the new number into the terminal, but once again, the error appeared.

"What's wrong with this thing?" Ovian asked.

"I don't know. Long range communications are one of those things that use a combination of science and magic. As far as I can tell, the technology is working fine. Maybe it's the magic that needs adjusting."

"Well, don't look at me."

"You just said your private tutor taught you about magic."

"Well, yes, but just because I know about bone magic doesn't mean I know how to fix it. That takes a goblin."

Radek let out a breath. "I don't really know how to use goblin computers, but I'm doing all right at it. Besides, do you have a better idea?"

Ovian glared at having his own words thrown back at him, but he pulled a handful of crystals out of his pocket and arranged them in a circle around the console. He went to stand in front of the viewscreen but glanced at Radek before starting.

"I'm not sure what you want me to do."

"Just look inside and see if you can find out why it's not working."

"You know mixing magics is dangerous, right?"

"So is trying to send a message to the elves from a secret goblin station. Are you going to do it or not?"

Radek sighed and started singing. Intermittently, light bloomed in the crystals, though it was never all at once, and it didn't last for very long. The terminal beeped and gibberish that looked like a combination of Elven and Goblin scrolled across the screen. Radek tapped the control panel. It squealed, but the display continued to only show nonsensical text. A faint acrid scent reached him, and he looked around, but couldn't find the source. It was only when he touched the control panel again that he felt the heat emanating from it. After a second, it was hot enough to burn. A thin curl of black smoke rose from the console, and sparks flew.

"Ovian, stop!"

The elf's eyes shot open. He gave Radek a questioning look just before the console exploded.

CHAPTER 16

Radek woke in a cold room. He was lying on the metal floor. He lifted his head and saw Ovian a few feet away. They were in a cell but rather than the magical shields of the elven prisons, the goblins used bars of black metal with spikes jutting from them. Dim red light gave off a faint hum overhead, and Radek couldn't see more than a few feet outside the cell.

He sat up and winced as pain shot through his shoulder. He touched it, and his fingers brushed against something hard. Radek yelped as agony surged in his arm. His hand came away with blood on it. Gingerly, he reached for his shoulder again and felt a jagged object. He clenched his teeth and gripped it. Tears welled in his eyes as he pulled the object out. He blinked several times to clear his vision and looked down. He was holding an irregular piece of metal, an inch long and dripping with his blood. He rotated his arm, and winced. It hurt a lot, but he seemed to have full range of motion. He examined himself. His robes could barely be called such anymore and were more holes than cloth. His left hand was red and a patch of skin had been melted off. He could barely move his fingers. Ovian wasn't in any better shape. He was on the ground, unmoving but breathing, and Radek limped over to him. The elf was covered in cuts and burns, bleeding a green substance that was closer to sap than blood. His pouch of crystals was gone. Radek tore pieces from his robe to make bandages, but it didn't do much good.

He sat down and leaned against the wall next his friend's still form. Everything hurt. Barely visible in the shadows, a pair of hanging guns pointed in their direction. One followed Radek's movement while the other stayed locked on Ovian. He closed his eyes as a profound regret welled up inside of him. They had failed.

He wasn't sure how long he sat there. Occasionally, Ovian would stir, but he never woke up. Radek opened his eyes when he heard the faint clank of metal on metal. It grew steadily louder until a goblin in an armored suit came out of the shadows. His nose was long, even for a goblin and his mouth looked like it had too many teeth. His leathery green skin was covered in warts and his red eyes almost seemed to glow.

"You're awake." He spoke in a low gravelly voice. The elven tongue sounded strange coming from him, and his pronunciation was just a little off. "I half expected you to die from your wounds. You still might, but since you're conscious, the Krom wants to see you. Get up."

Radek tried to lift himself off the ground, but pain surged through him, and he cried out. He slumped against the wall and shook his head. The goblin grunted and shoved an iron key in the door. He pulled it open and grabbed Radek's arm. With a sharp tug, he pulled him to his feet. Pain like Radek had never imagined tore a scream from his throat. The goblin pulled him from the cell and slammed it shut. He practically dragged Radek down the hall.

"Please," Radek said through tears. "Let me go slower. Stop pulling."

The goblin grunted but slowed his stride. Radek wished he had the pipe to lean on. Every step was agony, and it was all he could do to put one foot in front of the other. He stumbled more than once, but the goblin didn't slow. His captor led him to a lift. He pressed a few buttons and the lift rushed upward. Radek took several deep breaths and clutched his side, grateful for even this small break. Too soon, however, the lift reached its destination, and the goblin pulled him forward.

He wasn't sure how long they walked. The pain prevented him from keeping track. Eventually, they stopped before a door that slid upward. A white desk sat in the center of the room with a burly goblin seated at it. The guard threw Radek on the floor, and he grabbed onto the desk to avoid falling. It was only then that he realized the desk was made of bone. Instinctively, he backed up and tripped over his own feet. He cried out as he hit the ground. The goblin at the desk laughed.

"You may leave us, Grabune."

"But Krom..." the guard started, but the Krom banged his fist on the table. The sound it made sent shivers down Radek's spine.

"Do you think one injured human child is a threat to me?"

Grabune cross his arms over his chest. "No, Krom."

He backed out of the room and the Krom stood up and gazed down on Radek. "I expect people to stand in my presence."

The fear pheromone hung thick in the air, and Radek resisted the urge to look back toward the door. It took everything he had to meet the Krom's gaze.

"Sorry, this is about all I can manage."

His voice only cracked a little as he spoke, and the goblin sat back down. There was a beep followed by a series of words in Goblin, though the Krom spoke too fast for Radek to translate. A few seconds later, a pair of goblins carrying a metal chair entered. They put it in front of the Krom's desk and practically pulled Radek's arms out of their sockets as they forced him into it, not caring that he cried in pain. One of them was thinner and taller than the others had been, and Radek wondered if it was female though he couldn't see anything that would tell him one way or another.

The Krom glared at Radek. "I didn't know your people had the will to send children as spies. The elves have certainly been complaining to us about ours for a long time. Who sent you? Was it the humans or the elves? Or have they formalized an alliance? What was your mission?"

"What?"

"Who are you spying for, boy? I know you deleted data off the ship, for all the good that did. What else were you supposed to do?"

Radek stared at him blankly for a few seconds before shaking his head. "Nothing."

The Krom tapped a control panel on his desk. A transparent viewscreen rose up from a slot Radek hadn't seen. It flickered to life and displayed the cell Radek had been in. Ovian was still lying on the ground.

"I'm told your colleague isn't doing as well as you are." He looked Radek up and down and gave a half smile that showed sharp teeth. "Though that's not saying much. I can arrange for care to be given to him, if you will tell me your mission."

Radek stared at the images. Ovian hadn't moved. He could already be dead. He bit his lower lip before speaking. "I told you. We don't have a mission. We just want to get back to *Vanel*."

"If you don't have a mission, what were you doing on the *Krilock*? Or do you expect me to believe that you weren't the human who knocked out the repairman. I suppose it was someone else who burned through the floor of the engine room as well."

"We were just hiding." Radek's voice sounded desperate even to himself. "We had hoped that when the ship got where it was going, we'd be able to sneak out and find a way home."

"That still doesn't explain what you were doing in the ship in the first place."

Radek's eyes went from the Krom to Ovian. "If I tell you, you'll help him?" The goblin inclined his head, and Radek spouted out the first thing that came to his mind. "The elves wanted to sabotage your efforts to learn about dragon magic. They didn't want you to make a discovery first."

The goblin leaned forward. "Are they close to finding a dreadnaught? Or is it the humans? Is that why the humans wanted Halune? We knew it was in that general area but..." He didn't wait for Radek to answer and tapped a button on his console. "Dispatch a party to Halune." He glared at Radek. "How close are they?"

Radek stared at him, not quite able to believe his deception had worked. He could only shrug, and a grin appeared on the goblin's face. "Withholding information until I deliver on my promise? Very well. I'll dispatch a medical officer to your cell. He'll see to the worst of your injuries. I'll call you back when you're feeling better. Perhaps then, you'll be more talkative. If not, well," He ran a claw along the top of his desk, carving a thin line in the bone. "I'm sure I can convince you."

Once again, he spoke into his console, and a guard came in to drag Radek away. He wasn't sure if it was the same one who'd brought him here. This one didn't do Radek the courtesy of going slow for him, and by the time they made it back to the cell, he collapsed, no longer having the strength to keep himself standing. The pain barely allowed him to see. It took several minutes for him to gather the strength to crawl to Ovian. His friend was still breathing and he seemed not to have gotten any weaker. Thankful for that small bit of good news, Radek leaned against the wall and waited.

CHAPTER 17

The medical officer was a heavily scarred goblin with only one natural eye. The other, a mechanical replacement that looked more like a metal ball with a red light in it than an actual eye, hummed as its owner examined them. It had to be some sort of scanner, and Radek wondered if the eye had been lost in some sort of accident, or if the goblin had deliberately removed it in order to enhance his abilities. It would fit with what little he knew of the race, and the thought made him shiver.

The officer never gave his name. As soon as he came in, the two guards accompanying him pointed their weapons at Radek and Ovian. Then, they started chatting with each other, never removing their fingers from the trigger, and Radek envisioned one of them accidently pressing it and showering them with deadly blasts of energy. The medical officer jerked Ovian's arm up and, heedless of the fact that he now stood between the goblin guard and the prisoner, he used long nails to pluck out a piece of metal similar to the one that Radek had extracted from his own wound. After slathering a gel that smelled like rotten fish on Ovian's wounds, he turned to Radek. Again, his eye hummed and the goblin poked at Radek's shoulder. Radek screamed, and the goblin shoved a pill into his mouth. As soon as it touched his tongue, it began to fizz. The taste made Radek gag, and he tried to spit it out, but the goblin held his mouth shut.

The world spun and the next thing he knew, he was on the ground. Dimly, he was aware of the goblin working on him. The medic would regularly jab him with strange tools, but the most Radek ever felt was a gentle pinch every few seconds. He faded in an out of consciousness several times. The medic was usually there, but the last couple, he and Ovian were alone. Finally, he woke up and felt that some of his strength had returned. Ovian was lying next to him, though his eyes were open. Radek sat up. He still hurt, but it wasn't the incapacitating pain he'd felt before. Ovian blinked but didn't rise.

"Are you all right?" he asked.

"Don't know," Ovian said. "So hot. What's happening?"

"The communications terminal blew up, and we were captured." Radek put a hand on Ovian's forehead. "You're burning up." He thought for a second. "At least I think you are, but I'm not sure what normal is for you. Do elves have a higher body temperature than humans or lower?"

Ovian stared at him for a second before looking upward. Radek sighed. "Here, let me help you sit up."

Ovian groaned but managed to get into an upright position with Radek's help. He was sweating and seemed to have trouble keeping his balance. His hand fumbled at his waist.

"They took your crystals," Radek said. "Can't you do anything to heal yourself?"

Ovian shook his head, and the motion almost made him fall over. He put a hand on the floor to steady himself, and when he looked up, his face had a green tinge to it. "Healing myself is easier than healing someone else, but it's still complicated. Maybe if I had a crystal." He let out a breath. "Why is it so hot? I thought goblins liked a similar temperature to us."

"They do, Ovian. It's not hot."

Ovian blinked. "It's not?"

"No, I think you have a fever. Your wounds must've been infected."

"It's not that." Ovian brought a hand to his forehead. "My magic is out of balance. It's because I tried mixing it with the goblin's."

"I'm sorry."

"No, you were right. We had to try something." He took a deep breath and closed his eyes for a few seconds. "Sorry. It's just so hot. I'm going to try to cool it down. I know the song."

"If your magic is out of balance, should you be doing that?"

Ovian was already singing though. His voice was off and cracked several times. The song only lasted for a few seconds before he toppled over. The temperature dropped sharply, and Radek started shivering as his breath misted in front of him. He scurried over to Ovian and moved him to a sitting position. Ice had formed on the ground where he'd lain, his sweat having frozen. The chill only lasted a moment before the temperature returned to normal. Ovian opened his eyes after a few minutes.

"Sorry," he said. "It's hard to control right now. My head hurts."

"It's fine. Are you going to be all right?"

Ovian looked at the ceiling. "They say this kind of thing passes with rest. There are songs that help, but I should be fine without them as long as I can rest." He looked around. "That doesn't really seem too likely, though, does it? We have to get out of here."

Radek glanced at the guns. He wondered where the camera the Krom had looked into the cell with was, but he saw no sign. The camera would just be a minor problem if they got out. The guns, however, were another matter. One still tracked Radek while the other was locked onto Ovian.

"Your magic was a lot stronger," Radek said softly.

Ovian nodded. "I told you. It's out of balance. I can't control how much power I draw."

"Can you do it again? With fire, this time?"

"You want me to burn us?"

"Not us." Radek glanced at the weapons. "The guns, and maybe the lock so we can get out."

Ovian shook his head, though this time, he managed to remain upright. "I told you. I can't control it. I could just as easily create a spark that wouldn't do anything or a fire that would eat us alive. If I had been able to think straight, I never would've tried making it colder. I could've frozen our blood or drawn enough power to stop my heart." Radek stared at him for a second, and Ovian let out a breath. "No, I don't have a better idea. Stand back."

Radek moved to the back of the cell, and Ovian starting singing in his discordant voice. A small fire puffed into existence in the barrel of one of the guns, but it wasn't even as big as a candle flame. Ovian let out a breath and his shoulders slumped. The flame winked out. Ovian glanced at Radek, but before Radek could say anything, the elf closed his eyes and started singing again. At first, it looked like nothing was happening, but after a few seconds, the lock on the cell glowed a cherry red. Radek took a step toward it, but the heat drove him back. One of the guns followed him as he moved, but it moved sluggishly and had a watery sound. There was a spark and a curl of smoke rose.

"It's not enough," Ovian said, and the tune of his song changed.

Everything went dark and a few seconds later, dim red lights appeared overhead, providing just enough light to see by. The burning glow of the lock began to fade. Radek clenched his teeth and threw himself at the door. His leg gave out, but he managed to ram it. The weakened lock broke, and the door swung open. Radek closed his eyes and waited for the gun to fire on him, but it never came. He turned back to Ovian who was struggling to stand. Radek got to his feet and returned to his friend. His intention was to support Ovian, but they ended up leaning on each other as they stumbled out of the prison.

CHAPTER 18

Radek kept expecting guards to come after them, but they never appeared. A part of him hoped that meant no one had been monitoring their cell, but he knew that was too much to hope for. The corridor was curiously empty, and Radek eyed the hanging guns as they passed under them, but they didn't so much as twitch. Radek led Ovian to the lift he'd ridden. They stepped inside and looked at the buttons. They each had a goblin character on them. They weren't numbers though, and Radek was at a loss to say what they meant. He remembered which one the guard had used to take him to the Krom's office, and he was pretty sure he didn't want to go there.

"We have to get off the station," he said. "I don't suppose you noticed if the docking bay was near the top or the bottom."

Ovian closed his eyes for a second and leaned against the wall. "The ship moved up to get into the station, so it's probably on the bottom."

"You're right," Radek said as he hit the bottom button.

"Are you sure that will take us there?"

"No, but it makes sense." The lift started moving down. "That's a good sign, at least."

"What about the internal defenses?"

"I think you broke them. What did you do?"

Ovian gave him a weak smile. "Instead of fire, I used lightning. I didn't really think it would work. The station must not be complete for me to have that big of an effect."

"If you get this much stronger when you're sick, maybe you should stay that way."

The lift door opened, and they stepped out. Ovian stumbled, and almost caused both of them to fall. Even on this level, the lights were dim. What Ovian had done seemed to have affected almost the entire base. It was only luck that the lift had still worked.

Ovian shook his head. "The military tried to weaponize this. It didn't work. It's too unpredictable, and even if they don't end up drawing too much power, people who keep using magic when they're unbalanced only live a couple of days."

"And you still did it?"

"I wasn't really thinking straight the first time."

"What about the other times?"

Ovian bit his lower lip. "Goblin prisoners don't live more than a couple of days either."

They walked down a short hall and as they approached a large door, it slid upward revealing a cavernous chamber hundreds of feet long and at least that many wide. It must've taken up most of the bottom level. Dozens of ships of every size, from small one-man fighters near the center of the chamber to the mid-weight cruisers at the edge, filled the room. Suddenly, the red lights faded, and the standard lights blazed to life. After the darkness, they had to shield their eyes while their vision adjusted. Ovian's hand went to his ears.

"It's the alarm. I think they know we've gotten away."

"We need to take a ship. Maybe we can launch before they figure out how far we've gotten." Radek waved at the vessels. "Can you disable the internal defenses in one of these?"

Ovian shook his head. "Smaller ones don't have them though."

He indicated a craft that was five feet wide on one end and narrowed to a point ten feet away. It was probably a fighter of some sort. They went over to it, and it took Radek a second to find the panel on the side of the ship. He slapped a hand against it, and a hatch on the bottom of the ship slid open. An iron ladder lowered to the ground. Radek looked around, half expecting goblin guards run into the bay after them, but no one came, and they climbed into the ship where they found two seats, one behind the other. Ovian sat in the back. Radek tried to activate the controls, but nothing happened.

Suddenly, various doors scattered around the walls of the docking bay opened and dozens of goblins streamed out and started climbing into the ships.

CHAPTER 19

Immediately, Radek and Ovian ducked down to avoid being seen through the window of the cockpit. A thousand ideas ran through Radek's head about what he could do if they were discovered. Most were dismissed the instant he had them. They were weak, wounded, and unarmed. They wouldn't have a chance against even one goblin, especially not if they wore their armor. Fortunately, the hatch to their ship never opened. After several minutes, Radek dared to lift his head. All of the goblins seemed to be boarding the larger ships while leaving the smaller ones alone. Without warning, the control panel in front of Radek came to life. A goblin face appeared, and Radek's blood went cold. He cried out, but it didn't notice him.

"It's just a transmission," he said, relieved.

The goblin started speaking in Goblin. He spoke for several minutes while Radek and Ovian struggled to put together the message, but as fast as the goblin was speaking, they only caught a few words.

"Did he say something about a dreadnaught?" Even through Ovian's exhaustion, the fear in his voice was obvious.

"Probably," Radek said as he looked over his shoulder. "The

Krom mentioned that when he spoke to me. What's a dreadnaught?"

Ovian didn't answer. His face had gone pale and his jaw was shaking. Radek had never seen any elf so afraid. Elves were among the oldest races, and even their children supposedly knew many secrets. The sight of his friend so frightened made his blood go cold. With a visible effort, Ovian calmed himself enough to speak.

"Dreadnaught is the official class of ship, but almost everyone calls it a nova dragon. It's a dragon battleship." He took several deep breaths, and Radek guessed only part of that was due to his imbalance. "The stories say they didn't even need crews. The dragons could control them with magic alone. If the goblins found one..." Ovian shivered. "They would be more than a match for any one race. Maybe for any two."

"But it's only one ship," Radek said. "I saw an elven battle cruiser once. My father said it was strong enough to reduce a planetoid to dust. Don't you have a couple of dozen of those?"

"Fifty-three, I think," Ovian said as the ships outside began to power up. "You don't really understand. How much do you know about the dragons?"

"Not a lot," Radek admitted. "They had already left known space when humans built their first interstellar drive."

"I'm not talking about that. What do you know about them from ancient times, before the races left Earth?"

Radek thought for a second. "I've heard stories. Sometimes, they made whole kingdoms afraid. They were monsters."

"Some of them were," Ovian said. "Against those, entire armies were sent, and the dragon still won more often than not. Dragon battleships are as far beyond the ships of other races as dragons themselves are beyond an elf or a human. They could destroy entire fleets. If the goblins know where one is..." He took in a breath. "We can't let them learn how to use it."

On the other side of the docking bay, the larger ships rumbled. Now that the lights were back on, they could make out details. Ovian scanned them and uttered an Elven word Radek didn't recognize, though when Radek asked what it meant, the elf blushed. Instead of answering, he pointed to the largest ship in the bay. It took up as much space as any three ships. It was at least a hundred feet long and half as tall. Like other goblin ships, it was wide at the back and thinned at the front. Its hull would've been smooth if it weren't covered in weapons.

"It's a goblin capital ship. They're illegal under the Rageshian treaty. If they have one and are willing to send it out..." Ovian shook his head. "I was going to say it would be war, but they've already started one."

The goblin on the screen said the word dreadnaught followed by another word they both recognized. Radek looked over his shoulder at Ovian. The elf's jaw had dropped.

"Halune?" Ovian said. "The nova dragon is on Halune?"

"That's the planet my father was trying to get from your people."

Ovian nodded. "We never had more than a small outpost there, and even that's been abandoned. Is it possible we had a dragon ship under our noses this whole time?"

"Maybe they're wrong," Radek said. "The Krom didn't seem sure."

Ovian looked around. "They seem sure now."

Radek started to respond, but Ovian shushed him as the goblin continued. Radek struggled to understand.

"Vorluk and Lugin," Ovian said. "I don't know those words."

"They sounded like places," Radek said. "I think he said other ships are leaving from there. Do you think they have other stations built in elven space?"

"At this point, nothing would surprise me." Ovian closed his eyes for a second. "The goblins could attack the elves on three fronts. I have no idea how many ships they have, but that would've taken most of their fleet even before the war. If they've somehow rebuilt, we'd have to divide our forces to stop them. With our fleet occupied, they could send the nova dragon right for Droshala, practically unopposed."

"So what do we do?" Radek looked out over the ships and they slowly exited the docking bay. "Do you think we can use the communications on this ship to contact the elves?"

"No, when I tried to adapt the communications terminal on the other ship, I saw what was wrong. It has a like-to-like enchantment built in."

"What does that mean?"

Ovian let out a breath. "Don't you know anything about magic? Unless they're specially built to do otherwise, the transmitters that use bone magic can only send to receivers that use it too."

"But that's stupid," Radek said. "Why wouldn't they want to be able to communicate with other races?"

"Goblins don't really like other races. They only agreed to keep a Krom at *Vanel* after the war because we forced them to put that in the Rageshian Treaty."

The goblin capital ship rumbled across the ground and disappeared through a hatch on the floor on the other side of the docking bay. Radek stared at the opening for several seconds before looking back at Ovian.

"Then, we fly back to *Vanel*, or to Droshala and warn the elves. I think I can work the ship now that they've activated it. We'll tell the Droshalan council."

Again, Ovian shook his head. "What could we tell them? If my people ignore the goblin fleet to protect Droshala from the nova dragon, we'd be sacrificing every other planet we have. We have to get to Halune."

"But the goblins are already there, and we haven't exactly had good luck dealing with them. We're both hurt, and you're still sick."

Ovian narrowed his eyes. "The goblins won't stop with the elves, you know. The dwarves won't be able to stop them. The other races never maintained big enough fleets to be able to be a serious challenge. How long do you think it'll be before the goblins turn their eyes to the humans? They would love to return to Earth."

Radek bit his lower lip. "We could reach Treya. They could contact the elves, the dwarves, and all the rest. If we combined our fleets we might..."

Ovian was already shaking his head. "Maybe if we had a year, we could do that. You know as well as I do that the races never get along. Plus we'd have to convince them to listen to us."

"All right. So what do we do once we reach Halune?"

"Find the nova dragon first, if they haven't already found it. If they have, find some way to disable it."

Radek blinked. "That's your idea? Find a ship that's been hidden away for hundreds of years and figure out how to break it?"

The edges of Ovian's mouth twitched. "Do you have a better one?"

Radek shook his head. The ship started to vibrate and an alarm went off. Radek turned back to the display. The goblin had disappeared and letters flashed across the screen.

"The docking bay has been depressurized," Radek said. In front of them, ships retracted their landing struts and hovered before disappearing through the same hatch the capital ship had gone through. Radek looked back at Ovian. "I guess this is it."

The elf nodded and strapped himself in. Radek did the same, and pushed a flashing red button, hoping it was the activation. The ship rose into the air and Radek gripped the control stick. The goblin once again appeared on the screen, but this time, it saw them, and its brow creased in a scowl. It spouted out several words, but Radek didn't bother to try to translate. Instead, he pushed forward on the stick, and their fighter tipped forward and took off. It seemed to be on an automatic pilot because as soon as it reached the hole in the floor, it changed direction and shot downward. Radek and Ovian found themselves in space in front of the station and in the middle of a goblin fleet. The gas giant was like a great orange sphere suspended in space. The goblin on the screen vanished. A few seconds later, the fighter's alarms went off, and it only took a second to figure out what it meant. They were being targeted. A myriad of goblin voices came from the screen. They all spoke at once, their words tumbling over each other, though Radek did catch one word: surrender.

"You should probably activate the bone drive," Ovian said.

Radek tapped several buttons and flipped switches.

"I don't know how."

"How about weapons?"

Radek flicked a switch and a violet light shot forward. The voices from the command panel screamed.

"Those I can do," Radek said.

"I guess we fight, then."

"Fight an entire fleet?"

"Do you have a better idea?"

Radek let out a breath. "We fight."

CHAPTER 20

Radek pushed the control stick, and they shot forward between two larger vessels. Violet bolts of energy shot out at them, but the movement had apparently caught everyone off guard, because the shots went wide, though they did set off the proximity alarm. Radek twisted the stick and the fighter turned right so hard it momentarily overpowered the inertial dampeners, and they were pressed against the left side of the ship. The alarm beeped and Radek just had time to see that a shot had been fired before purple energy washed over the cockpit. The fighter rocked violently. Indicators on the control panel flashed yellow and orange, but Radek didn't have time to figure out what they meant.

The proximity detector showed a dozen smaller dots split off from one of the larger ones. A quick look over his shoulder revealed that the larger vessels had launched fighters of their own. Unlike Radek, those pilots actually knew what they were doing, and they were gaining fast.

"Try circling back to the gas giant," Ovian said. "Maybe we can hide in the upper atmosphere."

"Do goblin fighters work in atmosphere?"

"Yes," Ovian said. "Some of them."

"Like this one?"

"Radek, I don't even know what kind of ship this is. Do you think we have a better chance against..." There was a beeping sound as Ovian tapped his own control panel. "A million ships?"

"There aren't a million ships out there."

"Can you beat them?"

"No."

"Then, it doesn't really matter. Turn around, and stop flying so flat."

"I haven't figured out how to move up and down." He twisted the control stick, though he did it gentler than before. They went into a wide turn and headed back toward the fleet and the gas giant beyond.

"You'd better figure it out."

Radek clenched his teeth but didn't answer. He held down the weapon's control and a shower of purple lights spurted out in a wide arc. He mashed on the buttons, trying to figure out how to aim, but nothing happened. A few of his shots hit the incoming fighters, but they swerved out of the way before sustaining any serious damage. Radek shouted and banged on the console. He could fire the weapon, but without being able to aim, it didn't do much good. Even aiming wouldn't help much if he couldn't figure out how to activate the bone drive.

"Why haven't they destroyed us?" Ovian asked.

"Are you really complaining about that?"

"No, but you're not very good at this. They should've blasted us out of space within a few seconds."

"The Krom thinks we're spies," Radek said. "He probably wants to take us alive so they can question us and figure out why the elves sent us."

"But the elves didn't send us."

Radek bit his lower lip, glad that Ovian couldn't see his face. "Actually, I told him they did."

"What?"

"It was the only way he would agree to send someone to treat you."

The proximity detector beeped just as another impact rocked their ship. A fighter came up from beneath them, using the spray Radek had used, but to much greater effect. Nearly every energy ball hit their fighter. More of the indicators went orange, and a few flashed blue.

"Is blue bad?" Ovian asked.

"I think so."

Radek pushed the control forward, and their engine sputtered but didn't give any more speed. Two more indicators went blue. Another blast grazed their ship, and Radek was thrown forward, inadvertently tilting the control stick instead of pushing. The fighter pitched down and shot away from the rest of the ships. It took a second for him to gather his bearings before turning the fighter back in the direction of the gas giant, this time on a course that would avoid the bulk of the fleet.

"I think we're going to make it."

No sooner had the words left Radek's lips than a brilliant purple beam enveloped them, so bright they had to shield their eyes. The ship vibrated so hard Radek thought it would fall apart. He thought he heard Ovian singing, but over the noise of the ship, it was impossible to be sure. When the after image faded and they could see again, all the indicators went blue except for one which sputtered from blue to orange and back again.

"What hit us?"

Radek blinked and looked at his display, but it had gone dark. He looked up, and the station was pulsing with purple energy. "I think the station shot at us." He tapped the control panel, but nothing happened. "It completely overloaded our systems."

"What about that one?" Ovian pointed to the sputtering light.

"I don't know what that system is." He leaned forward and examined the letters, but they made no sense. "Sorry, deciphering goblin technical commands wasn't part of my lessons."

"Do you know how to activate it?"

"But I told you I don't know what the system is." Ships drew closer and Radek turned to look at Ovian who was giving him a level stare. Radek let out a breath. "No, I don't have a better idea."

He started flipping switches at random as the ships grew larger above them. Finally, the screen lit up. Numbers scrolled across it, but Radek didn't bother to try understanding them. There was a button just under the screen, and he tapped it. The universe went white and Radek was pressed against the back of his chair so hard he lost consciousness.

CHAPTER 21

R adek," a voice spoke from the darkness. "Wake up. Radek."
"Ovian?"

Slowly, his eyes opened to a sea of stars. He looked around, but the movement almost made him pass out again. He took several deep breaths, but he was nearly overwhelmed with nausea. He turned. Ovian looked pale in the light of his console and seemed to be having trouble keeping his eyes open.

"What's going on?" he asked, though the effort of speaking was draining.

"I think you activated the bone drive."

Radek looked at the display. All the indicators but one were still blue, and the one that wasn't flickered. A warning blinked on the display. Reading it made Radek's head hurt, and the letters swam in his vision. He had to try several times before he could get all the way through it.

"The drive is only halfway functional. Everything else is out, including life support. We only have the air that's already in the cockpit. The drive cut out because it couldn't form a connection to navigation. We've only gone about a light year."

"At least they're not shooting at us. Can we fix it?"

Radek tapped the screen, but nothing happened. He flipped switches and was able to get back to the screen that controlled the star drive. He kept looking, but couldn't find any sort of diagnosis screen so he went back to drive control.

"I don't see any way. Everything is broken. Even the status message was just the last thing generated before diagnostics went offline." He bit his lower lip. "Can you do anything?"

Ovian didn't answer for several seconds. His breathing was heavy, and sweat dripped from his brow. Finally, he shook his head. "I can't mix magics. At best, it will kill me. At worst, I'll blow up the ship."

"No, not the bone drive. Can you fix the rest of it? At least the navigation system?"

Ovian shook his head before going still. Radek wondered if he had passed out, but he opened his eyes a second later and gave Radek a sheepish smile.

"Sorry, no. Mechanical repair is almost as complicated as healing."

Radek undid his restraints and pushed himself up. Without the ship's artificial gravity, he floated up. Ovian's eyes followed him, and he raised an eyebrow. Radek propelled himself toward the back of the ship.

"Maybe there's something obviously broken, something we can fix."

Ovian looked like he was going to argue, but after a few seconds, he nodded and undid his own restraints. They found a panel in the back of the ship. Normally, it would've required specialized tools to remove, but it came off easily, having been held in place by an electronic seal that was no longer working. The skull of the bone drive was cracked, and the light shining from its eyes had been reduced to a dim glow. Most of the wires around it had been burned out and several had melted together. Only a few looked whole.

"What do we do?" Ovian asked.

Radek shrugged. "Switch around the damaged wires for the working ones, I guess. You do that, and I'll look at the indicators. Maybe I can figure out which one goes to which system."

Ovian nodded and Radek floated back to his seat. After a few seconds, all of the indicators went dark. He called to Ovian to undo whatever he'd done, and most of the lights came back. Radek leaned in close and examined the writing next to them, which was difficult with only the light of the indicators themselves to go by. After a few minutes, he was reasonably sure he knew which was life support. He guessed the one that had a word similar to 'map' was navigation. The blinking light was almost certainly the bone drive, and he had no idea what the rest might represent.

He spent the next few minutes on the bone drive screen. The numbers seemed to be coordinates and were set for somewhere in goblin space, but with his head fuzzy, he couldn't be sure. He wracked his brain, trying to remember the coordinates to Halune. Ovian was no help in that regard, having been a poor student of navigation and stellar geography. When he thought he had it, Radek started converting the numbers to the goblin system, though the lack of oxygen was making it difficult to concentrate, and he kept losing track of where he was in the conversion. He ran the calculation three times and got a different result each time. His fourth attempt got the same result as his second. He decided he wouldn't get a better answer and entered it into the system. By then, heat had leached out of the fighter, and he could see his breath. A layer of frost had formed on the inside of the cockpit windows. He was shivering, and he'd lost feeling in his hands. The light next to the 'map' word turned orange.

"That's it," Radek said. "Strap yourself in."

"It's fixed?"

"Navigation is fixed," Radek said through clattering teeth. "I think. I've locked in the coordinates for Halune."

"What about inertial dampeners?"

"I don't think so."

"I should try to fix those too. If we activate the drive without them..."

"I won't last much longer," Radek said. "It's too cold. Can you enchant another one of those crystals?"

There was a click as Ovian strapped himself in. "The goblins took all my crystals, remember?"

"All right. Brace yourself. If you wake up and I don't, push me out of the way and work the controls."

"I don't know how to fly this thing."

Radek quickly went over what he'd learned about the control stick. "If this works, we'll come out near a planet, but I don't know how close. If there's no one to control the ship, we could crash or burn up in the atmosphere. You have to try."

"All right," Ovian said. "I'm ready."

Radek nodded but remembered that Ovian probably wouldn't be able to see the gesture. His finger hovered over the activation button for a second. This wasn't going to be pleasant without inertial dampeners. It could kill them. Of course being stuck trillions of miles from anywhere with no supplies and no life support would kill them anyway, so it wasn't like they had a lot of choices. He took a deep breath and pressed the button. The ship's acceleration drove Radek back into his seat. Space around them turned white just before he passed out.

CHAPTER 22

Radek woke to the fighter spinning, his view alternating between the black of space above and the green of the planet below. He felt like he would throw up. All the indicators had gone dark. The one for the bone drive didn't so much as flicker. He grasped the control stick and pulled back, but the ship was completely unpowered, and it had no effect. They were spinning out of control, being drawn in by the planet's gravity.

"Ovian, wake up!"

The elf moaned and Radek shouted at him again.

"What?" The elf's word was long and drawn out. He probably hadn't even noticed what was happening.

"Sing, stop us from falling."

"But..."

The word was drawn out and faint, and it sounded like Ovian was going to sleep again. Radek looked over his shoulder. His friend was having trouble lifting his head and couldn't seem to keep his eyes open.

"You have to sing," Radek said. "If you don't, we'll crash."

"I can't..."

The word faded as music filled the fighter. Ovian's voice was pitched high, and it hurt Radek's ears. The ship lurched as it stopped spinning so suddenly a piece of the nose was torn off. Above them, green trees rushed by in a blur.

"We're upside down!"

"I'm trying."

The tone of the song changed as the ship slowly rotated until space was above them. The ship rocked and shook violently as they fell. Cracks formed on the cockpit window and heat poured in. Ovian cried out and the ship lurched. Radek looked back, but Ovian was unconscious and green blood dripped from a cut on his head. Radek mashed down on the control panel, hoping for any reaction, but nothing happened. He tugged at the control stick, but there was a crack, and it came free. Radek stared at it for several seconds before tossing it aside. He checked his restraints, but they were as secure as he could make them. He gripped the side of his chair and clenched his teeth. They passed through a cloud, and the ship rocked.

"Brace yourself," Radek cried out, though he had no idea if Ovian had woken up.

They tore through a green canopy, though they were moving too fast for Radek to make out any details. He could only watch in horror. At the speed they were going, crashing into a tree could easily vaporize the ship.

The cockpit grazed a branch, and the impact set them spinning. There were a series of bumps and crashes. Radek lost all bearings, and his head banged against the side of his seat. Suddenly, the ship bounced. There was a tearing sound and the cockpit shattered. Dirt and dried leaves rushed in, blinding him. He pulled them away from his eyes just as the front of the ship crunched against a large tree.

Sap poured over the front of the fighter, though the tree was so massive that the damage to it was minimal. The coppery taste of blood filled Radek's mouth, and when he spit, his saliva was bright red. Everything hurt, though after moving his arms and legs, he didn't think he'd broken anything. The pain in his arm had been raised to new heights, but he took it as a good sign that he could feel anything at all. He tried to undo the restraint, but the metal latch stuck. He looked over his shoulder. Ovian wasn't moving, and a trickle of blood dripped from his nose.

"Wake up," he cried out, desperately hoping his friend wasn't dead. "Please wake up."

He felt a prick on his hand though when compared to the pain the rest of his body was in, it was hardly noticeable. He looked down and saw a shard of glass near his fingers. He gripped it as carefully as he could and used it to cut away his restraints. It took him almost an hour to get through them enough to be able to get out. He crawled to the back of the ship, wincing at every movement. He put a hand on the left side of Ovian's chest but didn't feel a heartbeat. He panicked until he remembered the elven heart was situated on the right, nearly six inches lower in the chest than a human one, and when he placed his hand over the correct spot, he felt a thumping, weak, but undeniably there. Ovian's restraints came free much easier than Radek's, and he pulled his friend out of the vessel and onto the ground. It was only then that he took the time to examine his surroundings.

The forest was like none he'd ever imagined. The trees were like great slumbering giants. The one they had crashed into made even the ones the elves built their houses in seem like saplings. Radek couldn't even begin to guess how high it went. Entire city blocks could fit inside of its trunk. Some of the lower branches were wide enough that the fighter could've landed on them with room to spare. In contrast, the bushes near the base of the tree were tiny things, no more than a foot tall with leaves smaller than Radek's fingernails. He half dragged, half carried his friend away from the crash site and put him on a patch of soft dirt.

The ship was in ruins. It looked like little more than a disfigured hunk of metal. Its shape had been twisted beyond recognition, and Radek could hardly believe they had survived the crash. He hobbled back to its remains and climbed into the back, hoping to salvage the bone drive, but the skull had shattered. Only a few pieces were more than an inch wide, and there didn't seem to be enough to make a full skull. Either most of the pieces had been thrown free in the crash or they had been reduced to dust by whatever force had shattered the skull. A quick search determined there was nothing else worth salvaging, so he headed back.

By the time Radek made it back to Ovian, his friend's eyes were open and had a faint green glow to them. He held his hand to his forehead and didn't notice Radek until he sat down next to him.

"How are you feeling?"

"Strange." Ovian's voice sounded hollow and there was an echo so light Radek wasn't sure he actually heard it. "Did we make it?"

Radek looked around. "We made it somewhere. There are green plants, a blue sky, and a yellow sun. I'm not sure those are characteristics of Halune, though."

Ovian nodded, though for a moment, he couldn't seem to raise his head again. "We made it."

"Are you sure? Do you know the characteristics?"

"Not really, but what are the odds we randomly found another planet that can support us?"

Radek nodded. "Good point."

Ovian waved at a nearby bush. "Besides, look. That's a crystal tree. We always bring those to new worlds."

"You grow crystals on trees?"

"Not real ones. They're good enough to hold some enchantments, but nothing big." He started to rise. "I guess I should go see if there are any ready. It would be better than nothing."

"Stay there," Radek said. "I'll get them."

Ovian slumped back down and nodded. "You should be able to see through them, but they shouldn't be completely clear."

It was a struggle to walk to the tree over such uneven ground. He examined the branches for crystals but found none. He was about to turn around when a glimmer caught his eye on the lower bark. Apparently, sap dripping down the trunk had a tendency to congeal into crystal formations. Almost all of the ones on the bark itself were an ugly yellow color that was completely opaque, but he found a few that he thought might work. There were others on the ground, but most of those were completely clear and seemed to have started decaying. He scooped up the good ones and brought them back to Ovian who tore a piece of his own robe to make a small pouch while Radek sat down beside him.

"What do we do now?" Ovian asked when he'd stored the crystals.

Radek thought for a second. "I'll look around. You get some rest."

Ovian looked him up and down. "Are you joking? You're not in any better shape than I am."

Radek thought about the effort it would take to stand up and shuddered. Ovian cocked his head, but Radek shrugged.

"If I rest, I might get better enough that I can walk without limping. If you rest, you'll be able to use magic without risking killing us. Your singing is more important than my walking."

Ovian looked like he was going to argue, but his shoulders

slumped, and he nodded. Radek gritted his teeth as he stood up. He couldn't move very fast, and pain ran through his left leg every time he put weight on it. He walked for fifteen minutes, but all he saw were trees. Occasionally, the sun peaked through the branches. Radek still found it odd to have a sun that color. He had been too young when they left Earth to remember living there, and Sirusi, the star Treya orbited was white, and everything here looked just a little off. The air felt thick, and it wasn't long before he was covered in sweat. Briefly, he considered climbing a tree to see if he could get a better view but almost instantly rejected the idea. These trees were much smoother than the ones on *Vanel*, and he'd been uneasy about the thought of climbing those. Maybe when Ovian was better, he'd be able to, but Radek would probably kill himself if he tried. He looked down at himself and shook his head. He wouldn't kill himself. In his condition, he wouldn't even be able to get high enough to do himself any serious injury.

The sky began to darken as the sun neared the western horizon. At least, Radek assumed it was west. Nearly four out of five known planets rotated in the same direction, but that was no reason to assume Halune did. He didn't want to be wandering around the forest at night, so he headed back in the direction of the ship. Unfortunately, he'd never spent much time outdoors, and he hadn't been following a trail, so he had no way to retrace his steps. The night was far darker than he'd expected, and he could barely see a few inches in front of him. He walked even slower than his injuries required. It took him nearly two hours to find the spot where he'd left Ovian. His friend was snoring softly. Radek found a soft spot and made a pillow out of moss. His recent trials and ordeals seemed to come crashing down on him all at once, and he practically collapsed into sleep.

CHAPTER 23

Radek brushed at his face without waking up fully. There was a chirp, and he opened his eyes and screamed. The bird that had been sitting on his face flew into the trees. Radek stared after it, blinking several times. The bird had four wings and bright yellow feathers. It landed on a nearby branch and turned to him. It chirped several times, and Radek got the impression it was angry at him. He almost laughed as it flew away.

The sun shone through the branches, twinkling as it reflected off of dew covered leaves. Ovian was still asleep, and Radek stood up, crying out at the unexpected surge of pain. It wasn't just the cuts and burns. Every muscle in his body felt sore, and he spent several minutes limping around the area, trying to loosen himself up. Then, he started looking for something to eat. He found a tree with low hanging yellow fruit that, aside from the color, looked a little like a strawberry. He picked a few but didn't eat them. He worried they could be poisonous, but then anything could be poisonous here. Since the elves had had a base here, he was sure at least some of the local plant life had to be edible. Maybe Ovian would know.

He found a small stream nearby and drank, surprised at how thirsty he was. He splashed water on his face to wash away dirt and dried blood and looked for anything to carry water back to Ovian with, but there was nothing but rocks and trees. He sighed and cleaned himself off a little more before returning to Ovian.

This time, he'd made sure to keep track of where he'd come from, so getting back was much easier. A twig snapped under his foot, and Ovian's eyes snapped open. He blinked and looked at Radek as he sat up. Radek suppressed a feeling of resentment that Ovian didn't seem to be nearly as sore as he had been.

"How are you feeling?" Radek asked.

"Better." His voice still had that strange echoing quality. "I don't think I can sing yet, but I don't feel like I'm going to pass out." He looked down at his own wounds and winced. The sappy blood had crusted over. "Those hurt though."

Radek led him to the stream where the elf cleaned himself off. Radek showed him the fruit, and Ovian took a bite without hesitation. Radek gasped and Ovian cocked his head.

"What?"

"That could be poisonous."

Ovian's eyes widened, but his expression softened after a second. "You're right. It could've been. I don't know what I was thinking. I don't know what it is, but it's not poisonous. I'm sure of that."

"How can you be sure if you don't know what it is?"

Ovian brought a hand to his forehead and closed his eyes for a second. "I don't know." He pointed to one of the small leaved bushes at the base of another huge tree. "Those have roots that are edible too. I'm not sure how I know that, though."

Radek stared at him for several seconds before taking a bite out of the fruit. It tasted sweet and there was a faint hint of cinnamon. He ate three and went back to the tree to pick more. He made a makeshift bag out of some of the remains of his robe and packed several in there. He turned and lifted his hand to block the sun from his eyes. It had found a hole in the canopy of leaves and was shining at him. He thought back to the idea he'd had the day before and turned to Ovian.

"Can you climb trees?"

Ovian looked at one of the trees. He spent several seconds examining the bark before he looked toward the sky. "Maybe." He walked to one of the bigger ones and laid a hand on it. He made a face and pulled back. There was a sticky substance on his fingers. "Probably. The bark is smooth, but these trees have sap, and that always makes climbing easier. It takes forever to wash off, though."

"I think you should try. Maybe you can get a better view of the surrounding area. We might even be close to that outpost you were talking about." Radek grinned. "I can help you wash your hands later, if you want."

Ovian scowled at him and his eyes scanned the canopy for a few seconds. "You realize I'll only be able to see a few miles, and that's only if I can get above the canopy. Halune has something like two hundred million square miles of land."

"You can remember that, but you can't remember the coordinates?" Ovian looked at the sky, and Radek sighed. "We don't have any idea where we are except that we're probably on the right planet. We have to learn something, and you can see farther from a tree than we can if we just wander around."

"All right. I'll try."

He put a hand on the tree in front of him and paused for a second. "Strange," he said, but before Radek could ask what he meant, Ovian scrambled up several feet. He paused again. Radek called after him, but Ovian didn't answer. Instead, he moved up, stopping every fifty feet or so, though he didn't seem to be struggling. After a while, he disappeared into the upper branches. Radek waited, but Ovian didn't come back. He called out but got no response. He wasn't sure how long Ovian had been gone, but it had to be at least an hour. Finally, he tried climbing the tree himself. In spite of how easy the elf had made it seem, Radek couldn't even get a grip. Something tapped him on the shoulder, and he practically jumped out of his skin. He spun around and lifted his fists only to drop them when he saw Ovian standing behind him. The elf wore the widest smile Radek had ever seen on him.

"Where did you come from?"

"Over there." Ovian pointed to a tree about twenty feet away.

"How did you get on that tree?"

"I jumped."

Radek looked from one tree to the other. "You jumped all that way? I thought you were sick."

"I didn't jump directly. I went through four or five before I reached that one."

"So you're not feeling weak anymore?"

"No, it's the strangest thing. As soon as I started climbing, I felt better. The higher I got, the stronger I felt."

"Are you better then?"

"I think so."

He lifted his robes to examine wounds, and his eyes went wide. His burns had been replaced by pink skin, and his cuts looked several days old. His bruises had vanished entirely.

"What happened?"

"I'm not sure," Ovian said. He closed his eyes for a second. "Actually, I think I've heard something about this. My tutors said our magic is stronger on a planet supporting life, but I haven't actually been on a planet since before I started singing. I feel strange, like I've come home."

"Can you do anything about my wounds?"

Ovian reached forward but hesitated. "I wouldn't want to try."

Radek nodded. "Did you see anything up there?"

Ovian looked at the sky. "Not really. There's a hill a few miles to the east. We might be able to get a better view from there."

"How do you know it's to the east?"

"It's where the sun is."

"But how do you know the sun rises in the east on this planet?"

Ovian let out a breath, and his eyes darted around. "I forgot human use magnetic north to determine directions on a world. We use the sun. It makes things a lot easier. No matter what direction a world is rotating, the sun rises in the east.

"Fine, I guess it doesn't really make much of a difference. We'll go east."

Ovian started at a fast pace, but slowed down when Radek lost sight of him. Even then, Radek was having trouble keeping up. He was breathing heavily before they had gone a mile, and he had trouble keeping his feet from tangling with each other. After the third time he'd fallen, Ovian slowed even more and allowed Radek to lean on him. Birds chirped and rodents with green fur jumped from branch to branch. Once, they heard a growl belonging to some predator. They exchanged glances, but it seemed to be far off. There was nothing they could do about it in any case, so they went on.

Just before midday, the forest went silent. It was a change so abrupt that the pair noticed it right away. There was a high pitched whistle above them. Through a hole in the canopy, they saw a goblin fighter pass over them. A few seconds later, they heard the sound again, though this time, they saw no ship. Over the next several minutes, they heard dozens of ships, though only a few were visible through the trees. Though the pain was still intense, Radek forced himself to walk faster. When they finally made it to the top of the hill, Radek stared out over the forest. The sky was filled with goblin ships, and they descended into a clearing that was already packed with vessels.

"At least that answers one questions," Radek said in a voice barely above a whisper. "We are on Halune, and if that many goblins are here, the nova dragon has to be here too."

CHAPTER 24

Thy don't know where the nova dragon is," Ovian said.

"Why do you say that?"

"I told you. Dragons didn't need crews to fly their ships. If the goblins had already found it, they would only need a few to crew it. The only reason they would send so many is that they haven't found it. They're still searching. We have to find it first."

"Where do we look?"

Ovian glanced up. "I have to get back into the trees."

"You can't. It's too dangerous. The trees are probably shielding us from the goblin scanners. If you get higher, they might detect you."

"Goblins sensors aren't that good. They won't be able to tell me from those big dog creatures."

He didn't seem to be joking. "What big dog creatures?"

Ovian looked at the sky. "I ran into a family of them in the trees. They're all over the place. They look a little like apes but with sharp teeth and claws."

He was halfway up a tree before Radek could answer. He didn't want to call out for fear that the goblins would hear him, though the possibility that they were nearby was slim. Ovian didn't go all the way up, and even then, he just stared at the bark. He scampered down after a few minutes.

"They're spreading out," he said. "There are at least two hundred of them out there."

"How do you know that? You didn't even look."

Ovian turned away and spoke softly. "The trees told me."

"The trees?"

Ovian nodded. "It's strange. Ever since we got here, I've been hearing voices in my head. At first, I thought it was because I was still unbalanced, but it was even louder when I woke up. I didn't realize where the voices were coming from until I started climbing."

"You're hearing the trees?"

"I think so."

"Can all elves do that, or is there something special about the trees on this planet?"

"It can't be this planet," Ovian said. "If there were something that special about it, we never would've been willing to give it to your people."

"Well, if it's an elf ability, why didn't you know about it?"

Ovian looked to the sky. "I've been in space most of my life. My tutors talked about native magic, the magic that comes from a living world, but I didn't really listen. I always thought I would follow my father as the Veelan of *Vanel*. I never thought I'd actually be on a planet. I've heard elves talk about how the forest speaks to them. I just didn't think they were being literal."

Radek gave him a level stare. "Haven't you been to Droshala?"

"To Ralem." Radek cocked an eyebrow and Ovian's eyes darted around. "It's the capital city. Everyone there lives in trees, but those are cultivated by elf magic. I've never been in any place so..." he waved at the surrounding forest, and his next words were almost reverent. "Wild. It's different from anywhere I've ever been."

"Is there anything else you didn't pay attention to?"

Ovian looked at the sky. "If I wasn't paying attention, how would I know if they said it?"

"I would just hate for you to have an ability to find hidden dragon ships and you not know."

Ovian's eyes darted around. "I think if my teachers had mentioned anything about dragon ships, I would've listened. Besides, elves have been here for centuries. They would've found it if we could do that."

"Assuming they knew to look."

Ovian was about to answer, but suddenly, he turned and stared into the forest. After a few seconds, he motioned Radek, and disappeared into the trees. Radek went after him and caught sight of him before too long. Ovian stopped and Radek moved in next to him. He was about to ask a question, but Ovian tapped the top of his ear, and it took Radek a moment to remember it was the elven equivalent of putting a finger in front of your mouth to ask for silence. He nodded and followed Ovian through the thick underbrush.

After a minute, the faint sound of the goblin language drifted from where they'd been, and his blood went cold. He found himself looking into every shadow. Once, he saw eyes looking back and he grabbed at Ovian's robe, and the tattered cloth tore free. Radek gasped, sure anyone nearby would've heard the sound. Ovian looked back and Radek pointed, but at that moment, one of the four winged birds flew out of the bush. Radek yelped then started laughing. Ovian glared at him, but it only lasted a second before the elf joined him in his laughter. They both stopped when the leaves rustled, but Ovian put his hand on a tree and smiled.

"It's nothing, but we can't stay here long. The goblins will be here soon."

CHAPTER 25

They moved through the forest for a few hours before Ovian stopped in front of one of the city block sized trees and started to sing. Radek held his breath and got ready to catch his friend if he should fall, but all signs of the imbalance seemed to have been healed by his time in the forest. In fact, though the words still vanished from Radek's mind as soon as he heard them, they sounded somehow truer than any song he'd ever heard an elf sing. Slowly, the bark of the tree parted as if it were a curtain, revealing a large cavity inside. The walls glittered like gold as the sun reflected off the sap drizzling down onto every surface.

Ovian smiled. "It's the song my mother and her builders used to make our homes in the trees."

Radek nodded and followed Ovian inside. The ground was sticky and the air smelled minty. Ovian sang, and the bark closed behind them, plunging them into darkness. Ovian's song echoed strangely in the enclosed space, and a few seconds later, a hole appeared in the bark above them. It was surprisingly cool inside, and Radek touched the wall and pulled back a finger covered in sap.

"How long do we stay here?"

"A day. Maybe two. We'll wait until the goblins search this area so we don't have to worry about them."

"Couldn't we hide closer to the hill?"

Ovian looked up. "Maybe, if that's where we were going."

Radek looked at him. "Do you know where the nova dragon is?"

Ovian closed his eyes and put a hand on the wall. He shook his head and withdrew his hand, heedless of the sap covering his fingers. "I'm not sure. I know where something is. It's not natural, but it could just as easily be the elf outpost or some other landing sight the goblins are using."

"But it could be the nova dragon."

"Maybe."

"How far is it?"

"About five miles."

"You can detect something that far away?"

"Not exactly. I mean I know something is there, but I can't sense it. It's like when you see the sky light up in the east just before the sun rises."

Radek narrowed his eyes. "I don't think that actually makes sense."

Ovian let out a chuckle. "Try to imagine how I feel."

"Are the goblins heading in that direction?"

"They're heading in every direction, and they're moving too slowly to have an actual destination in mind. They're still searching."

"How..."

Ovian raised a hand and Radek went silent. They heard the muffled sound of goblin voices, but they went away after a few seconds. Ovian still held his hand up though, and the silence stretched on. Finally, Ovian let out a breath.

"There are search parties everywhere. We'll have to keep quiet."

"Why? They can't open the tree, can they?"

"Not with magic," Ovian said. "Probably not, anyway. They have blasters, though."

A muffled sound from outside silenced Radek, though he couldn't tell if it was a goblin or a wild animal. Ovian tapped the top of his ear and Radek nodded. They spent the rest of the day talking for a minute or two followed by long stretches of silence. Ovian's perception of the outside wasn't perfect, or rather, the trees' perception wasn't perfect. They couldn't tell one being from another, and they had only a vague notion of size, so Ovian couldn't tell if the things he sensed outside were animals or goblins. It was only by guessing which beings moved unnaturally that Ovian was able to have any idea of where the goblins were. By the time the sun faded from the hole above them, the elf was on edge.

"They haven't found it. They came close half a dozen times. One group even set up camp near it, but I don't think they've found it."

"Is it safe to go out now?"

Ovian reached for the bark, but pulled back before he touched it. He sighed. "I don't know why I keep thinking I need to touch it to speak to it. No, I don't think it's safe. All of the dog apes are hiding in branches. There's something else out there."

"Can you be more specific than 'something else'?"

Ovian shook his head. "Not really. I just have what the trees tell me. It's big, bigger than almost anything they've ever encountered, aside from themselves. They say they've felt it before, but not in a long time. This one," he tapped a wall and rubbed the sticky substance between his fingers, "was only a sapling the last time. They say it's been asleep since then, and they're scared. I didn't know trees could get scared."

Radek stared at him. "You don't think it's a dragon, do you?"

"The dragons departed from known space."

Ovian spoke the words automatically, but almost immediately, an uncertain look came over him. Radek pursed his lips. He had been taught the same thing. Everyone knew the dragons had left, but they were looking for a dragon ship, so who knew what else could be out here?

"We don't really know where they went, though, or why. Maybe they returned to their ships to sleep or something, and this one woke up when the goblins started looking."

Ovian bit his lower lip. "We should be so lucky."

"How would that be lucky?"

"If there's a dragon guarding the ship, it can probably fight off the goblins by itself, and we won't actually need to do anything. We don't really need the ship. We just need to stop the goblins from getting it. I don't think we can count on that though."

A roar pierced the night, and the forest erupted in sound as creatures clamored to get away. Even the tree vibrated and drops of sap dripped down. Their shelter had muffled the sound, and Radek could only imagine how loud it would've been outside.

"We're safe in here, right?"

Ovian shook his head. "That really depends on what you mean. If it really wanted to come in, I'm not sure anything could stop it. It's still far away, though, and it's probably not looking for us, so I think we're safe enough. We should get some sleep. It's not heading in this direction, and you'll need all the rest you can get."

"I just hope it doesn't come closer."

"Me too."

CHAPTER 26

The night passed in spurts of uneasy sleep and fearful wakefulness. The ground was sticky and uncomfortable. A couple of times, the creature's roar shook the tree, though it never got closer than the first time. Gradually, the light coming through the hole brightened, and the sounds drifting in from outside shifted as the nocturnal animals sought their dens. Ovian sat up.

"We should get going."

"Is the creature gone?"

Ovian shook his head. "It's been going after the goblins all night. At least, I think it's the goblins. It's still hunting them as far as I can tell."

Radek bit his lower lip. "At least if it's going after them, they'll be too distracted to come after us."

Ovian nodded and sang the tree open. The forest was strangely quiet, as if the creature's presence had frightened everything else into silence. A twig snapped under Radek's foot, and he was sure it could've been heard a mile away, but no goblins rushed out to take them prisoner, and eventually, he let out a breath he hadn't realized he'd been holding.

They moved at a snail's pace. Every once in a while, Ovian would stop and tap the top of his ear. Several seconds of agonizing silence would follow. Once, goblins came close enough that Radek could see their green skin through the bushes. They weren't doing a very good job of searching the forest and didn't notice the pair. After a few hours of walking, Radek noticed Ovian constantly looking over his shoulder.

"What's wrong?"

"It killed a lot of people here."

He pointed to what Radek had assumed was just a peculiar growth on a nearby bark, but when he looked at it closer, he realized a piece of metal had been embedded in the tree. Sap had flowed over it, and in another day or so, it would vanish beneath the layer completely. There was a dark spot on one end, and if Radek squinted, he could just make out the insignia on the metal that indicated its owner's division. It was goblin armor. His mouth went dry. Now that he knew what to look for, he saw other places where objects had been thrown into the trees by something with great strength. One particularly large bump was covered by dried leaves and had flies buzzing around it. The object was as big as Radek himself, big enough to be an elf. Or a goblin. He didn't get close enough to confirm his suspicions, though.

"Can you tell where the creature is?"

Ovian shook his head. "I think it can fly."

"It can fly?" Radek's voice was high pitched, and he put his hand over his head as if that would protect him from whatever this was. He realized what he was doing and put his hand down again. "And you're sure it's not a dragon?"

Ovian paled a little and looked up. "Whatever it is, it's not among the trees anymore. It just vanished. The only way it could do that is if it went above them."

"If it can fly, it has to be a dragon."

"No, I don't think so."

"Why not?"

Ovian motioned at the tree with several sappy lumps on the trunk. "There's no burn marks."

Radek tried to swallow, but his mouth was completely dry, and it took him a second to work moisture back into it. "Can you climb a tree? If it's flying around, maybe you can see what it is."

Ovian gave him a level look. "Do you want to go looking for this thing now?"

"No, I guess not. It would be nice to know where it was, though."

Ovian nodded. "As long as it stays away from us, it's fine with me. Come on. The other thing I detected is this way."

"Can you tell what it is now that we're closer?"

"Not really. I know it's underground. There's something there that's blocking the roots of the trees. It's not the outpost, though. That was built on the surface."

They continued to walk for the next few hours. Though it was still the middle of the day, the forest seemed darker. Radek found himself peering into every shadow, though even he couldn't say if he was looking for the creature or more goblin remains.

They came upon a steep incline. Ovian started to walk up it, but stopped after a few feet. He bent down and buried his hand in the carpet of leaves. He closed his eyes and sang.

"What is it?" Radek asked.

"We're here."

"It's under the hill?"

Ovian's eyes roamed over the area a head of them. He took a deep breath. "I think it is the hill."

Radek blinked at him. "Are you sure? It would have to be

enormous."

Ovian was moving his hands through the leaves and didn't turn to Radek as he spoke. "You don't know the half of it. It feels like this hill formed over the top of it. It goes down a long way, farther than the reach of the roots around its edge. This thing is huge."

"So it really might be the nova dragon."

"I think so."

Suddenly, a deafening roar came from above and a shadow obscured the sun. Radek looked up and saw wings so big they almost seemed to cover half the sky. The next thing he knew, he was running, pulling Ovian by the arm. The pain in his wounds was excruciating, but he ran on. Before he'd gone very far, however, there was a loud crack and branches fell from the sky. The creature landed so hard the ground shook. Radek fell and found himself staring at claws as big as he was. He looked up at the reptilian body. Its serpentine neck swiveled toward him and burning red eyes stared at him. A growl came from the creature's belly. Radek backed up and realized he was still holding Ovian's hand. They both got to their feet slowly. The creature's eyes never left them.

"That's not a dragon," Ovian said.

Radek shook his head. It was the same shape he'd always imagined a dragon to be. Its bat-like wings and long tail could've come out of one of the elven history files, but unlike the creatures he'd seen images of, this thing was made of stone. No, this was no dragon. This was a dragon golem.

CHAPTER 27

The golem roared so loud the power of it lifted Radek off his feet and threw him back. He slammed into the ground, right on his injured shoulder. His world exploded in pain. Ovian also flew back, but the elf managed to keep his feet under him as he landed. The golem lumbered toward Radek. Its stone foot came down, and Radek rolled away, the claw catching the edge of his robe. The material of the garment was already tattered, and it tore free easily. Radek got to his feet just as the golem snapped at him. He cried out and fell back, its stone jaws missing him by inches. Suddenly, Ovian leapt on the golem's neck. The creature seemed not to notice and lowered its head toward Radek. Then, Ovian started singing.

The golem roared. A chip of stone flaked off its head. The golem's neck lashed around. Its steps shook the forest as it tried to throw its attacker off. Ovian stopped singing, but he held on. The golem slammed into a nearby tree, reducing the lower branches to splinters. A shard embedded itself in Radek's shoulder in almost the exact spot the exploding console had wounded him, and he cried out. The next thing he knew, Ovian crashed into the ground next to him. The golem stared down at them, its eyes shining so bright it hurt to look at them. Ovian held up a crystal and sang a single word. The golem's eyes locked on it, and Ovian threw it to one side. The golem watched as it fell to the ground. The elf stood up in front of Radek and held his hand over his wounds. He sang, and pain surged through Radek. The world went red, and when his vision cleared, he saw Ovian, once again on the golem's neck nearly fifty feet away. His own pain had receded somewhat, though he seemed to have lost all feeling in his left arm. Ovian kept singing and another chip of stone flaked away, but it was no larger than Radek's fingernail. At that rate, it would take a year to destroy the golem.

The sun glinted off gold where the rock had been chipped away, and it shone just a little too brightly. Understanding dawned on him. Of course there would be gold. Just like elven golems had crystal eyes that enabled them to exist for long periods of time without being recharged, gold had to be a part of any lasting dragon construct. Ovian couldn't affect dragon magic directly, but maybe Radek could do something close.

"Ovian! I need a heat crystal."

The noise the golem was making as it thrashed through the woods was too loud. He waved at the elf but caught the attention of the golem instead. It thundered toward him. One of the trees it had damaged groaned and started to topple. Radek pointed to it, and Ovian's eyes went wide. He jumped off the golem and ran to one side. Radek tried to follow, but he couldn't lift his left leg. He dragged it behind him. The golem started to follow him, but Ovian threw another lure crystal, momentarily distracting the beast. The crack from the tree must've been heard from a hundred miles. The tree, as tall as a small mountain, crashed down onto the golem, driving it into the ground and uprooting a dozen lesser trees. Its trunk missed Radek by less than a foot, and the force of the impact drove it several feet into the ground and shook the earth, causing Radek to lose his balance.

Ovian came up next to him and offered him a hand up. "Are you all right?"

"I can't feel the left side of my body."

"Sorry about that. I told you healing was hard." He looked at the tree. "That won't hold it for long."

"I need a heat crystal."

"Why?"

The ground shuddered. "It uses gold magic. I was able to use the heat from the bone drive and combine it with your crystal to melt the metal on the goblin ship. Maybe I can do the same for the gold powering the golem."

"But the golem isn't generating any heat." Radek glared at him, and Ovian sighed. "No, I don't have a better idea."

He pulled out a crystal and started singing. As soon as it flashed red, the golem roared and dirt and splinters exploded upward. The golem was still half buried but was clawing its way out. Radek took the crystal and shoved it into a pocket on his robe, the only one that was still intact.

"Can you get me on that thing? I can't move fast enough."

"I'm not sure. My magic isn't working as well as it should on it." He looked Radek up and down. "You won't be able to climb it with only one good arm. Hold on."

He held his hand toward Radek and sang. A vine from the fallen tree shot out and wrapped itself around his chest. One end plucked a crystal from Ovian's hand, and the vine entwined itself, forming a tentacle with the crystal at its base. Radek gaped at it and looked at Ovian.

"It'll help you grip the golem so you won't have to use your hands." He turned to the golem. "Let me see what else I can do to help you get there. Are you ready?"

"Ready for what?"

Ovian had already started singing, and before Radek had a chance to ask anything else, another vine, this one with its end attached to a branch above, dropped and wrapped itself around him. He cried out in surprise as it lifted him into the air. The golem's eyes followed him up, but a second later, it turned its attention to Ovian who was darting back and forth between the trees. The golem lunged forward, but Ovian jumped out of the way. Radek flailed, but he had no control over the vine and could do nothing but dangle in the air.

Ovian ran right toward the golem. Radek cried out, but the elf threw a crystal into the air as he dove beneath the golem's legs. Its eyes locked on to the crystal and Ovian rolled to his feet before looking up at Radek and smiling. Radek's eyes went wide just as the vine holding him up loosened. He fell right onto the golem's back, and the enchanted vine that was still around his chest wrapped itself around the creature's neck and kept Radek from falling down.

As if the weight of Radek on its back snapped the golem out of a trance, it lifted its head and roared so loud that Radek half expected his brains to dribble out of his ears. It flailed violently, trying to throw him off, and if not for the vine tying him on, it would have succeeded.

Inch by inch, Radek crawled up the golem's ridged neck, the vine acting like a third arm that was much stronger than the other two put together. He reached the head, and the golem roared again. Instinctually, he covered his ears, trying to block away some of the sound. When the roar subsided, he pulled the crystal out of his pocket and jabbed it into the exposed gold. He searched within himself for any sign of the pulling sensation he'd felt when he'd used the heat from the goblin bone drive, but there was nothing.

The golem thrashed, but the vine held Radek on. He shoved the crystal in deeper, and it sank into the gold as if it were made of water. Radek felt a surge of energy run through him, and he gasped. He didn't have time to climb back down. He tried to throw himself, but the vine held him. He tugged at it, but it was too strong. He pressed it down into the stone and concentrated. He wasn't sure if it was his imagination, but he thought he could feel the power flowing through the plant, and he pulled at that energy and shoved it into the same pathways as the magic pulsing in the golem. The power mingled, and a few seconds later, the vine turned to dust. The crystal that had given it life was nowhere to be seen. Radek leapt from the golem and could almost feel its gaze fall on him. He crashed into the ground, and the pain blossoming in his left side told him that he was regaining feeling there. He rolled to his feet.

"Run!" he cried out.

"What?"

"Run! Get as far away as you can. I don't know how big it'll be."

"How big what will be?"

"Remember when you tried to change the goblin communications console?"

Ovian's eyes went wide. He threw another lure crystal and ran to Radek and grabbed his arm. The elf started pulling him forward.

"I'm out of crystals," he said.

"Hopefully, we won't need anymore."

The golem looked back at them and took a step forward. Its red eyes turned blue for a second before shifting back to their normal color. It opened its mouth, and orange light glowed within. For a moment, Radek worried that he'd somehow combined elven and dragon magic to create a statue that could actually breathe fire, but no flames erupted from the golem's maw.

Pieces of stone fell away and the gold beneath glowed bright orange. A drop fell on the ground and Radek expected it to burn, but it seemed not to have melted, at least not in any normal way. It had simply turned into a golden liquid and it covered a small patch of grass. The golem took another step forward. Its eyes brightened and cracks spread across its face. It lunged forward to bite, but missed them by several feet. The jaws closed with a crash, expanding the cracks on its head. Orange light glowed between them, and before the golem could take another step, its head was engulfed in an explosion. It didn't extend far enough to touch Radek and Ovian, but they felt the impact in the air. The golem crashed to the ground. Radek and Ovian stared at it for several seconds, neither saying anything for a long time.

"What do we do now?" Radek said eventually.

"We find where it came from."

"I think it's safe to say it came from the nova dragon."

"But if we're right, and the nova dragon is buried under this hill, the golem had to come out somewhere. That will probably give us a way in that's easier than digging."

"Good point. I don't suppose the trees can help us with that."

Ovian pursed his lips. He looked at the fallen tree for a second before walking to one that had a wide gash on its trunk. Sap ran down it, but Ovian ignored it as he placed his hand on the bark and closed his eyes.

"There's a tree that's not a tree over there." He pointed up the hill.

"What is that supposed to mean?"

Ovian looked at the sky. "I only know what the trees know. It's not a tree and won't communicate with me, but there's something that's a little like a root that goes directly into the nova dragon."

"A little like a root?"

"I don't know. It's too straight to be an actual root though."

Now that his adrenaline had worn off, Radek became acutely aware of just how much pain he was in, and it was an effort to walk. They inched up the hill until they came to a tree that looked exactly like all the others. Ovian put his hand on it but drew back almost immediately.

"It's a tree," he said, "but it's also not. I don't really understand."

"Can you open it?"

"I think so."

Ovian sang a few words, and the bark quivered but didn't open. He closed his eyes and his bow furled in concentration. He tried again, and this time, the bark parted revealing a cavity inside that looked little like the one they'd spent the night in. The wood was completely smooth, and there wasn't even a drop of sap. Most of the floor was dominated by a large hole, easily big enough for the golem to fit through. Radek walked up to it and peered down, but he saw only darkness.

"This goes all the way down?" he asked.

"I think so. Do you see a place we can climb?" Radek shook his head. "I don't think dragons had much use for stairs."

Ovian nodded and touched the wall of the hole. "I can probably climb down. It's rough enough to give me a good grip. I'm not sure how you can get down, though."

"I can try to climb."

Ovian glared at him. "You weren't that good of climber before. Now you're hurt and can't feel half of your body."

Radek waved his left hand at the elf to show that it was feeling better, but after a few seconds, he sighed. "Can't you sing to a vine or something and get it to let us down like you did earlier?"

Ovian started to shake his head but paused. "Actually, I think I can do that. I just never bothered because we all like climbing. Hold on."

After a few seconds of singing, a vine dropped out of the darkness above them. It wrapped itself around Radek, and he had to suppress the urge not to shiver. Another entangled Ovian, and Radek quirked his eyebrow. Ovian looked skyward and the vine around Radek loosened his grip.

"I have to keep singing or it'll let you go," Ovian said. "It's hard to sing while I'm climbing something like this." He tapped his foot on the ground near the hole. "This way, I can keep it up until we reach the bottom."

He started singing again, and Radek's vine tightened. It lifted him off the ground and began lowering him into the darkness. Ovian's singing echoed above him as they descended into the dragon ship that had lay hidden for centuries.

CHAPTER 28

They hung in darkness for what felt like hours. The air was thick with humidity. Radek was sweating profusely, and as he stared into the darkness below, he shivered and realized only part of his sweat was from the heat. He wondered if the vine would reach its limit before they got to the bottom. He was about to ask Ovian about it, but he remembered what the elf said about having to keep singing. Far below, a yellow light came to life. As they neared it, other lights appeared. They seemed to be in a tunnel of some sort. The walls were covered in dirt, but in some places, the dirt had fallen away, revealing a smooth metallic surface. Radek's heart beat faster. This had to be it.

Abruptly, the vine stopped. Radek looked down, but the darkness beneath them was barely held back by the string of lights running down the wall. If he squinted, he thought he could see the ground. There seemed to be a flickering somewhere below. The lights weren't bright enough to illuminate anything other than the wall itself, and Radek could barely see Ovian, though the elf was only a few feet away.

"I think I can see they ground. Is elven night vision better than human?"

Ovian kept singing but grabbed his vine. Radek could just see him nodding. Ovian stopped singing and the vine loosened. Radek felt himself start to fall. Full feeling seemed to have returned to his left side, and he gripped the vine as hard as he could.

"It's a bit worse, I think," Ovian said. "I can't see anything."

"Do you know the song that guard used to slow our fall?"

"I'm not sure I can maintain it. My magic dealing with plants seems to be stronger here, but distinct forces were never my strong suit, and you're already hurt. There is something I can try. How far down do you think the ground is?"

"I'm not sure. I can barely see it. It's not very far beyond those lights."

"They go on forever as far as I can tell."

Radek thought for a second. "About as high as my quarters were in the tree."

"That's about two hundred feet. Four seconds. Hold on."

"What..."

Suddenly, Radek was falling. He screamed and gripped the vine harder, but the vine was falling too. He imagined himself slamming into the ground and breaking every bone in his body, but before he'd reached the ground, his fall slowed and then stopped. The ground was only about five feet below him. The vine loosened, and he fell. His knees buckled when he hit the ground, and he gritted his teeth against the pain, but he managed to stay on his feet. A few seconds later, Ovian scurried down the vine and landed lightly beside him. Radek could just make out his face in the darkness.

"What did you do?"

"I made your vine detach from the top. After two seconds, I tied it to mine and tightened it so it would slow your fall."

"What if gravity here was stronger than on *Vanel*? I would've fallen faster, and you might not have stopped me in time."

Ovian bit his lower lip. "I didn't really think about that. I guess it's a good thing it wasn't."

Radek's mouth dropped. "You could've killed me."

"But I didn't. I don't see what the problem is."

"You promised to stop almost killing me."

Ovian furled his brow. "You know, I don't think I actually promised that." Radek glared at him and Ovian sighed. "Fine, I'm sorry for almost killing you again. Can we go now?"

"Go where?"

Ovian looked around, but the area was still dark. As soon as he took a step though, overhead lights came to life. They were in the middle of a large domed room. Silvery metal formed the floor and ceiling. Above them a hole big enough to accommodate the dragon golem was illuminated by faint yellow light. The ground immediately around them had mounds of dirt that had fallen from above. Three clawed footprints had been pressed into the ground. Radek knelt down and traced one of them with his finger.

"I guess this is where the dragon came from." He looked around. "Let's go check the wall. There has to be a door here somewhere."

Ovian nodded. They walked to one side of the room. Radek had to resist the urge to wince at every step. Though it had been short, the fall to the ground had reopened his wounds and undone whatever little healing Ovian had worked on him. They reached the wall, and Radek laid a hand on it. It felt warm, and there was a faint vibration.

"I think the ship has been activated."

Ovian looked at the lights overhead. "I think that much is obvious."

"No, I mean..."

He grabbed Ovian's hand and put it on the wall. The elf's eyes widened slightly and he nodded. He slid his hand along the wall. Radek did the same and moved in the opposite direction.

"I think it's getting stronger over here," Radek said.

Ovian nodded and walked over to him. "I could barely feel it where I was."

After another few minutes, they'd gone a quarter of the way around the room. The wall dinged, and a square under his fingers lit up. The wall hummed and a crack appeared in front of Radek. It widened until it had formed a door fifty feet tall. A wide hall stretched out before them. The ceiling was well above them and was dotted with overhead lights that looked like miniature suns embedded in the ceiling. Radek and Ovian exchanged glances.

"If this was built for dragons, why would they have a panel that would activate at our height?" Radek asked.

Ovian looked at the ceiling. "Some of the stories say the dragons had humanoid servants. There are always those willing to bow down to power, and some dragons were great forces for good in the galaxy."

"That makes sense. I don't guess you know anything about the layout of a nova dragon?"

Ovian shook his head. "We don't have a lot of records about the dragon ships, and my father doesn't have access to the information we do have. It's too highly classified."

"Do you think we'll have to worry about internal defenses?"

"I have no idea. I'm not sure how powerful gold magic is, but it could still be strong enough to provide power to those systems even after all this time of being inactive." He bit his lower lip. "That is, assuming the golem wasn't all they had."

"That was more external defenses, don't you think?"

"Good point," Ovian said. "Let's be careful."

Radek rolled his eyes. "Thanks for reminding me. I would've never thought to be careful if you hadn't mentioned it."

Ovian glared at him as they came to a three-way fork. "Which way?"

"Aren't you the one who said if we don't know which way to go, one way is as good as another?"

"I also said we should be careful. Do you have any idea?"

Radek shook his head. After a few seconds, Radek turned down the left hall. Ovian caught up with him before he'd gotten very far. Eventually, they came to a long hall with dragon-sized doors lining either side. Radek picked one at random and walked up to it. He placed a hand on the door and it hummed. There was a muffled ding. A few seconds later, there was another. Radek heard a whirring sound. Shortly after, the door slid upward.

The room inside was huge. A pile of gold coins as tall as he was covered nearly half the floor. It gleamed in the overhead lights and almost seemed to have a life of its own. Radek stared at it for a second and remembered the old stories that said dragons slept on their treasure and wondered if that was more than a story.

Nearby was a smaller, humanoid bed. A large screen on one wall came to life. A translucent dragon with blue scales appeared. It spoke in a language Radek didn't know. The voice sounded vaguely feminine, though he couldn't say why he thought that. He looked at Ovian who shook his head. The image changed to a second language that was just as incomprehensible as the first.

"I'm sorry," Ovian said. "We don't understand."

The dragon looked at him. Its next words came out in elven.

"You are not recognized as part of the crew. State your intentions."

Radek and Ovian exchanged glances. Radek hadn't really been sure dragons could speak, though he had to admit it made sense. Still, he would've never guessed a dragon would sound so ordinary. It had an odd accent, like someone who was speaking the language for the first time. Radek nodded to his friend and stepped forward. The dragon focused its gaze on him.

"We're here to stop the goblins from taking over the ship."

"There are no goblins on this ship," the dragon said.

"No, but they're looking for it. If they find it, they might be able to take control of it."

The dragon's eyes glowed white. "Are you an acolyte?"

"A what?"

Its eyes narrowed. "Which dragon do you serve? Which one informed you of my location? What are your master's access codes?"

Radek looked back at Ovian who looked at the ceiling. He turned back to the dragon. "We don't serve any dragon. We found the ship on our own."

"You are the ones who destroyed my intruder repellent?"

"Your intruder repellent? Don't they belong to the ship?"

"I am the ship."

Radek looked around. The lights pulsed a little and made the pile of gold seem to come alive. He looked up at the dragon.

"You are the ship?"

"I am Trakor, avatar of this vessel. Did you destroy the golem?"

"We had to. It was trying to kill us."

The dragon bowed its head. "Its detection systems malfunctioned two hundred years ago, and there was none here to repair it. Its loss is regrettable though not entirely unexpected. I have been without crew for a long time. Are you the ones sent to replace them?"

Radek looked at Ovian who only glanced at the ceiling. Radek

139

nodded.

"Yes," he said. "Yes we are. Do you know where the goblins are?"

"There are no goblins on the ship. External sensors do detect a number of life forms not indigenous to this world. Some are moving toward the access cavern to this ship. Readings suggest, though do not prove, they are goblins."

"That's them. Can you stop them?"

"External defenses have been disabled." The dragon narrowed its eyes, and Radek shuffled his feet.

"Yeah, sorry about that. How about hiding? Is there any way you can avoid detection?"

"The cloaking field has been active since I was buried here. Additional countermeasures can be deployed if necessary."

"Yes." Radek seized on the suggestion. "Additional countermeasures. Use those."

"Deadly countermeasures require input of a level red access code."

Radek glanced at Ovian. "I told you all of our records about dragons are classified. I don't have an access code."

The dragon's eyes intensified and he snorted. "If you were the first of my new crew, you would have an access code."

"You don't understand," Radek said. "The dragons are gone. They left known space a long time ago."

"Yes, that is known, however it is irrelevant. If you do not have access codes, you may not activate primary or secondary systems. Tertiary access will be granted provided you are not seen as a threat to the ship."

"What's tertiary access?"

"Non-protected files. Layout of publicly available area. Ships logs that do not contain classified information."

"Ship's logs," Radek said. "Show us those. Maybe they'll help us figure something out."

The dragon vanished and a series of incomprehensible symbols appeared. Radek stared at them before looking at Ovian who glanced at the ceiling.

"Translate to Elven," Ovian said.

The screen shimmered and the curved characters of the elven language replaced the jagged ones that had been there before. Ovian turned to Radek who shook his head.

"I'm not sure. All the computers I've used operated by touch, but I can't reach that one."

In response to his words, a small screen they hadn't noticed came to life near the ground. It mirrored the larger one and Radek scanned the list of files. They were organized with the earliest entry at the top, so Radek tapped the one on the bottom. The list disappeared and a dragon with shimmering green scales appeared on the screen. He started speaking in a language that seemed to be more growls than words. His voice was deep, and Radek had the sense that this being was terrible in anger.

"Can you translate to Elven?" Radek asked.

The image shimmered, and the sound faded to be replaced by Trakor's voice.

"*Trakorki* has been successfully buried on Grantor. No sapient life is present, but the ship's energy patterns have been cloaked as a precaution. The heavy vegetation on the surface should provide additional protection. Three security golems have been left with instructions to deter any potential discovery using nonlethal means."

"That didn't work out too well," Radek said.

Trakor's image returned. "The security golems malfunctioned."

"Right," Radek said.

"Do you wish to see the rest of the log?"

"Yes, go on."

"Estimated time for the reliable function of the golems is somewhere between five and eight hundred years. To protect any who may stumble upon this world after the expected degradation of the command, a timed deactivation command has been entered, though it is unknown if this will last without maintenance. *Trakorki* is the last ship to be hidden in this sector. The rest of the crew has already retreated to the sanctuaries among the stars. Command codes have been set in case we ever return, though high command thinks this to be unlikely. This will be my final entry. Captain..." A series of roars and grunts followed that apparently had no translation. "Signing off."

The captain vanished.

CHAPTER 29

"Well, that didn't tell us much," Ovian said.

"I know. I was hoping for a little more." Radek spoke to the screen. "Is there anyone besides the dragons who had the command codes?"

"That information is classified."

"Of course it is." He sighed. "Does this ship have enough power to take off even though it's buried?"

"Primary and secondary functions cannot be accessed without a command code."

Radek let out a breath of frustration. "I'm not asking you to take off. I'm asking if you can. Give me ship status. Is that a tertiary function?"

The screen flickered for a second. Ovian sat down on the pile of gold, and a coin rolled away and stopped when it hit Radek's foot. Trakor glanced at the elf but addressed Radek.

"It is. Engines are powered down, but the shaping on the gold drive remains viable. Compartmental power system is operational. Power routing system nonoperational. Shield power remains sufficient to burn away soil covering this vessel, though such an act will burn most of the available power. Secondary weapon power operational. Primary weapon power nonoperational. "

"Primary weapon?"

"*Trakorki*'s primary weapon is a phase burst cannon generating sufficient heat and radiation to pierce the crust of a level quanti type world and release the mantle onto the surface."

Radek and Ovian exchanged glances. "You mean it can destroy a planet?"

"The phase burst cannon cannot destroy an entire planet, though it can render the surface of a rocky world uninhabitable by most non elemental life forms."

They both just stared at the screen for a long time before Ovian broke the silence. "We can't let the goblins get this ship. They'd head straight for Droshala. Nornir wouldn't be far behind. With both the elven and dwarven homeworlds gone, there would be nothing stopping them from taking over the galaxy."

Radek's instincts were to speak up in defense of the human fleet, but he caught himself. With the help of the elves, the humans were just now starting to become a significant power in the galaxy, but nova dragon or no, there was no way they'd be able to stand up to one of the major races.

"At least they don't have the command codes either," Radek said.

"Are you so sure?"

"Not really. Anyway, that weapon is disabled."

"What if it can be repaired?"

"I was taught goblins can't use gold magic."

"We don't know anything about gold magic. Maybe they can reroute the power from other systems."

Radek turned to the screen. "Is that possible? Can the power be rerouted?"

"Power routing system is nonoperational."

"Can it be done manually?"

"Power can be routed manually, however none of the currently active systems have enough energy to power primary weapons."

"Not even the star drive?"

The screen flashed to a map of the ship. A room toward the back was flashing and yellow lines ran from it to the back of the ship, giving the image the appearance that it was moving. After a second, Trakor reappeared and focused on him.

"The gold drive operates on an integrated power source that cannot be routed away."

"There," Radek said. "You see?"

"Can they use another power cell?" Ovian asked.

"The inactive power cell can be replaced with one of sufficient charge."

"And that would let the goblins use the primary weapon?"

"If the goblins had command codes, replacing the power cell would allow them to fire the weapon."

"We can't let that happen," Ovian said.

"We don't even know if they have a power cell," Radek said.

"Are you willing to bet on that? They won't stop with the elves. Are you willing to risk Treya? Earth?"

That made Radek take in a sharp breath. He shook his head. "No, I'm not. Can the primary weapon be destroyed?"

"That information is restricted."

"But it can be repaired."

"Yes."

"Can you show us how?"

"But we don't want to repair it," Ovian said.

"If we know how to repair it, we might be able to figure out how to destroy it."

A map of the ship appeared on the screen. One room was flashing green and had two red dots in it.

"I think that's us," Radek said.

"Correct," Trakor's voice said from the screen. A room in a different part of the ship started flashing as well. "This room contains the inactive power cell. If it is replaced, the weapon can be brought online."

Radek nodded at Ovian and headed for the door. It was something, at least. After all, they had both destroyed objects created by other races by combing alien magic with that of the elves: Ovian with the goblin communication console and Radek with the golem. Granted the effort had nearly killed them both times, but still, the plan was better than nothing. Probably.

CHAPTER 30

The lights of the hall lit up as they approached, almost like miniature suns lighting up a vast canyon. Each of the circular lights on the ceiling had to be at least a dozen feet across. Radek felt like an insect walking through a giant's house. Once, they were about to turn, but a screen lit up on the wall, and Trakor's face appeared, informing them that they were going the wrong way.

"That's weird," Radek said. "She has to know we're going to try to destroy the weapon. Why is she helping us?"

Ovian looked at the ceiling. "It's a magical construct. It doesn't 'know' anything. It's been programmed to answer certain questions. It's a good one, so it can probably even make intuitive leaps to figure out how to give you what you want. If you ask it how to get to the power cells, it will tell you. It can't choose to keep that from you just because of what you'll do when you get there."

Radek nodded, and they kept following the avatar's instructions. It took longer than he expected. With the ship designed for creatures so much bigger than they, the distances displayed on the floor plan were deceptive. He could scarcely imagine how big the ship actually was, though he suspected half a mile long was a conservative estimate. It didn't help that the dragons seemed to have been averse to straight lines. They had to wind through several side passages, and more than once, they couldn't take a path because it required flying. It was a full hour before they'd reached a large set of double doors. They slid apart. A light flickered above, revealing a room with a large pile of gold bars, though the metal seemed somehow dimmer that Radek had expected. It was like it needed to be polished, but he knew that wasn't the case. At one end of the room, a circle on the wall shone brightly. Radek went to the gold and reached out to pick up a bar. As soon as he touched one, he drew his hand back. It felt cold, almost icy. Ovian quirked an eyebrow.

"What is it?"

"I'm not sure." Radek shivered. "I think I can feel the missing magic."

"You can do that?"

Radek shrugged. "I guess so." He looked at the circle on the wall. "I think that's where it connects to the rest of the system. Give me a crystal."

Ovian patted his robes. "I used up the last of them keeping the dragon away from us."

"Can you try to do something to it?" Radek asked. "Like you did to the goblin commutation terminal?"

Ovian narrowed his eyes. "The one that blew up?"

"Yes."

"That would be dangerous."

"More dangerous than letting the goblins get this ship?"

"Good point."

Ovian placed his hand on the circle and closed his eyes. He sang, and the circle began to glow. Sweat beaded on Ovian's brow. His song wavered, and the circle flared and let out a screech. Ovian's song gave way to a scream, and the elf grabbed his head in between his hands. Radek went to his side. When Ovian looked up, blood was dripping from his nose. He brushed some of it away with his hand and stared at his fingers for several seconds before shaking his head.

"It's shielded somehow. I've never felt anything like it."

"Are you going to be all right?"

"Yes, just give me a second."

"Trakor?" Radek called out.

A screen appeared on the wall. "Yes?"

He pointed at the circle. "This is a conduit of some sort, right? It sends power to the other areas of the ship?"

"You are correct."

"Is it shielded against the magic of other races?"

The dragon inclined its head. "Yes. Mixing magics can be volatile. All sensitive areas of the ship are similarly protected."

Radek let out a breath. "What do we do now?"

Static flashed across the screen for a second before Trakor reappeared. "I have no orders regarding any instructions to give you."

"I wasn't talking to you," Radek said as he looked at Ovian.

"Where are the goblins?" Ovian asked the avatar.

"Goblins entered the ship twenty minutes ago," Trakor said.

"What?" the two said at once.

"Goblins entered the ship twenty minutes ago," Trakor said in exactly the same tone as before.

"How did they find the ship?"

"A hole was detected in the tree above the access tunnel. The goblins found it and climbed down vines into one of the golem storage chambers."

"Oh no," Ovian said. "I left it open. I even left the vine to give them easy access. This is my fault."

"Let's worry about that later. If they want to repair the weapon, they'll be here soon. We should get out of here." He turned to the screen. "You said 'one' of the golem storage rooms. Are there others?"

"Yes. Three dragon golems were set to guard this ship. Two were properly deactivated after five hundred years."

"Are there ways out in those rooms too?"

"Yes."

"Can you show us a way that avoids the goblins?"

"Yes."

Radek nodded, and they left the room. Following Trakor's guidance, they wound through the ship. A few times, they heard footsteps echoing down the hall, but they never got close. Eventually, they came to a large circular room like the one they had entered the ship through. A stone dragon stood in the center with its wings outstretched. Its eyes were black, and it didn't move. Aside from not trying to kill them, it looked exactly like the one they had faced before. There was a large hole in the roof of the chamber, though it was too dark to see what lay beyond.

"Do you have any idea how we get up that thing?" Radek asked.

Ovian shook his head. "I could try singing vines down, but they're probably too high to hear."

Radek eyed the golem. "What if we activate that?"

"Are you crazy?"

"This one didn't malfunction. It deactivated just like it was supposed to. If we can activate it, maybe we can get it to fly us to the surface or even to fight off the goblins. Trakor, can we do that? Can this golem be reactivated?"

"Overriding the deactivation command requires access to secondary commands."

Radek sighed. "So much for that idea. Is there any way we can get out?"

Trakor inclined his head. "Localized artificial gravity can be engaged in reverse at a level just above the gravity of this planet to lift you through the access corridor."

"Does that require secondary access?"

"No, systems used to exit the ship are tertiary functions. Do you wish to exit the ship?"

"Yes."

"Step to the center of the room, near the golem."

They did as they were told. Radek couldn't take his eyes off the statue. He kept expecting it to eat them, but it remained lifeless. As soon as they were in front of it, there was a ding, and they began rising into the air. It was a strange sensation, more like they were falling that flying. Of course technically, that was exactly what they were doing. Their hair lifted up, and Radek could feel the blood rushing to his head.

Once again, lights came on as they entered the corridor leading to the surface. Radek looked down as the ground was swallowed in darkness. After a minute, they stopped rising. It was a little painful as their bodies were pulled between the reversed gravity generated by the ship and the natural gravity of the planet. They were beyond the reach of the lights in the ship, so Ovian started to sing. The air slowly illuminated, though Radek knew it wouldn't last for long without a crystal to house the magic. They were in another tree, its bark as bare of sap as the one they'd entered the ship from. The tone of the song changed, and a gentle gust of wind blew them toward the edge of the hole they were floating in. The light dimmed as Radek reached out and grabbed the edge. He pulled himself up and heard scuffling as Ovian did the same. After a second, the song went quiet.

"This is another one of those trees that isn't a tree," Ovian said.

"That makes sense, if they're really hiding the entrances to the ship, the dragons probably put them there. They're probably the same kind of tree. Can you open it?"

"I think so."

He had to sing for almost a full minute before a slit appeared in the bark. The sun was nearing the horizon as they stepped out. Immediately, Ovian moved toward the closest tree and touched it. He closed his eyes for a few seconds. Then, they shot open.

"We need to get out of here."

"Why?"

"The goblins are coming out of the other tree. They're spreading out. I think they're looking for us."

"How would they even know we're here?"

"They know someone opened the tree and let down the vine." Ovian cursed. "Trakor. He told us when the goblins were coming. He would give them the same kind of information."

Before he could respond, they heard a voice yelling in Goblin. They looked at each other for a second. Then, they ran.

CHAPTER 31

With Radek's injuries, the uneven ground was much more difficult to move in than the than the smooth floor of the ship. They were halfway down the hill when Radek's knees gave out, and he tumbled down several feet before slamming into a tree. Ovian was by his side in an instant, pulling him to his feet. They tried to run, but his legs didn't seem to have the ability to move right. He'd been able to manage on the relatively smooth ground of the ship, but outside, his wounds reasserted themselves. He shook his head.

"Go. I'll tell them you went in the other direction. Maybe you can get away."

"I'm not going to do that. Hold on."

He started to sing, and vines dropped from the tree and wrapped themselves around both of them. Their squeeze sent renewed pain through Radek, and he cried out. Ovian tapped the top of his ears, and Radek forced his screams back. The vines lifted them into the trees, though the pain they caused brought tears to Radek's eyes. Eventually, they deposited the pair on a wide branch. Radek doubled over and breathed heavily. It was several seconds before he was able to sit up straight. Ovian was by his side.

"Sorry," he said. "I couldn't think of what else to do."

"Couldn't we have just hidden inside a tree again?"

"I didn't want to risk it. They already know the entrance to the nova dragon was hidden in a tree. They might start looking inside others too. At least, up here, we can move around if they find us."

Radek tried to stand, but the pain kept him down. "You can move around, you mean."

Ovian laid a hand on the branch they were sitting on. "You'll be fine. The goblins don't know where we went. They're scattering...wait. There's a group gathering at the base of this tree."

He pulled back and winced. He looked down just as a red flash came from below.

"What is it?" Radek asked.

"They used their blasters on the tree. They must think we're hiding inside." He replaced his hand on the tree. "We need to get to another one." There were tears in his eyes. "This is an old tree, and it should be allowed to meet its end with dignity, not like this." Ovian shook his head. "It can't take much more damage. It'll fall if they keep this up."

Radek nodded and struggled to his feet. The branches of the trees were interwoven so that they could almost walk directly from one tree to another, and Radek leaned on Ovian as they moved to another branch. Radek wanted to sit, but Ovian shook his head.

"These trees are too close together. When one falls it takes a lot of the nearby branches with it. We have to move farther."

Even with Ovian's help, Radek could only manage a slow limp. The branches behind them vibrated, and a sweet burning smell wafted from below. There was a sound like thunder, and the ground beneath them tilted and vanished. The branches they were standing on shook violently, and Radek fell. He clung to the branch. If it had been thinner, he might have fallen off, but this branch was wide enough to land small ships on. There was a cracking sound behind him as part of the branch fell away. Radek imagined himself falling and landing among a group of hostile goblins, but he knew that was ridiculous. If the branch he was on broke away, there was no way he would survive the fall. Fortunately, what remained of the branch stayed steady. It took several seconds for Radek to calm down.

"What are they doing now?"

Ovian gave him a weak smile. "The tree fell on some of them. I don't think they expected it to go down when it did. The forest is in mourning, though. One of them doesn't die very often." He shook his head. "No, that's not true, but these trees die slowly. It's rare for one of them to die all at once. Now, there's been two in a single day. They're...I'm not sure sad is the right word, but I can't think of one that comes closer."

"Fine, but what about the goblins? Do you think they'll find us?"

For a moment, Ovian looked angry that Radek didn't seem to care about the trees, but finally, he let out a long breath and shook his head. "Probably not. They haven't shown any indication of searching the upper levels." He put a hand on the branch again. "Oh, that's strange."

"What?"

"They're running. Some are going back into the nova dragon, but most are trying to get away."

"Is there another golem out? Did one get reactivated?"

"I don't think so. The trees aren't detecting anything like the last time." The branches vibrated, though there was no wind to shake them. Ovian's eyes went wide. "Oh no. Run."

"I can't run."

"We have to get off this hill."

"Why?"

"The trees are detecting movement beneath them. They all are. This..." He motioned to the vibrating braches. "is because the ground is shaking. The goblins have activated the nova dragon."

"How?" Radek asked. "They don't have the command codes."

The branches started shaking harder. Ovian sang and vines lifted Radek and tied him to Ovian. The elf struggled under his weight, but he managed to keep his feet. He ran with surprising speed, leaping from branch to branch, not seeming to be thrown off balance by Radek's weight at all. Creatures Radek hadn't been aware of appeared and started running alongside them. They had long arms and hair that was closer to gold than brown. Their elongated faces reminded Radek of a dog, but their hands were closer to an ape. Once, when Ovian stumbled, one of the creatures caught him.

The canopy was alive with movement as birds and rodents tried to get away. The earth itself groaned as a hum filled the air. Orange light flickered beneath them, and the smell of burning vegetation mixed with an oddly sweet odor filled every breath. Radek could just make out the fire through the carpet of branches. Ovian leaped just as the branch he'd been standing on lifted. A few seconds later, it fell away as the tree it had been attached to tumbled off the ship. Ovian kept running until they were a hundred yards away. Only then did he turn around and go silent. Radek realized he'd been singing the whole time, and as soon as he stopped, the vines tying the two together came loose.

Trakorki lifted into the air. There was still a thick coat of dirt on top of it, but it was smoking as it pressed into the shimmering yellow light forming the ship's shield. A tree fell, and as soon as it touched the bubble of energy, it burst into flames. Radek's jaw dropped. The ship was made of a silvery metal that shimmered in the sunlight. It was crescent shaped with a long straight section extending from the middle of the curve, making the whole ship look vaguely ax-shaped. With nothing to maintain scale, it was easy to overlook the sheer size of the ship as it rose higher into the air. Radek's original estimate of half a mile was ridiculously low. That thing had to be miles long, and they had explored only the tiniest fraction. It vanished into the sky leaving Radek and Ovian staring.

CHAPTER 32

"We failed," Ovian said.

The wind blew through the canopy. Most of the fires started by the nova dragon's shield had gone out. The damage to the forest actually seemed to be minimal, except for the massive hole the departing ship had left. Radek could still see signs of animal life. It seemed odd that creatures so small could be so resilient. If they could do it, why not him?

"We haven't failed. Not yet."

"What do you mean 'not yet'? The goblins have activated one of the most powerful ships ever built by one of the most powerful races ever to inhabit the stars. It would probably take the combined power of most of the races to stop it, but to do that, they would have to first know the ship was coming. We couldn't even warn the elves. They'll be caught completely by surprise."

"The ship isn't fully operational yet," Radek said. "Remember, Trakor said there were a bunch of systems that didn't have power anymore."

"Yes, but all they need is a new power cell."

Radek rolled his eyes. "How many dragon power cells do the elves have?"

Ovian absently plucked a leaf as big as his head from the ground and began tearing it. It released a vaguely minty scent. "None."

"Then, what makes you think the goblins have one?"

Ovian looked to the sky. "Well, they had the command codes."

"Having codes and having a magical material are two very different things. Maybe we can still stop them."

"How?"

"I don't know. The first thing we have to figure out is how to get off this planet. There's an old elven outpost here, right?"

"Yes."

Radek motioned to the ground where the rumbling had subsided. "Well, let's go. Maybe there's a ship or something there."

Ovian shook his head. "We have no idea where it is, though. It could be on the other side of the planet. Besides, we wouldn't leave a crystal drive just lying around, especially if we're planning on giving this planet to the humans."

Radek nodded and pursed his lips. "We could go to the goblins. We know they brought a bunch of ships here. We even know where they are. It's not like we haven't stolen one of those before."

"Then what?"

"I don't know. Maybe we can figure out where they're going. We don't actually know how fast a nova dragon is, especially one that hasn't had maintenance in a couple of centuries. Maybe we can go faster and warn everyone about it."

Ovian bit his lip and nodded. He looked Radek up and down. "Are you sure you're up to it? You're in pretty bad shape."

"Maybe I can do something about the gold magic." Ovian narrowed his eyes and Radek shrugged. "I know. I can't think of what that would be either, but I have to do something. Anyway, it doesn't matter what shape I'm in. I have to go."

"All right. We'll travel on the tops of the trees to avoid notice. Maybe enough of the goblins left on the nova dragon that they left their own ships unguarded."

Radek nodded and they headed back in the direction of the goblin landing field. It was like a whole different world up here. Radek had assumed that all the trees were of the same species, but they weren't. The leaves varied in both shape and size. Even the bark had different textures. Some were sticky under his feet while others were so slippery even Ovian had to slow down, though all had branches that were big enough for them to walk easily on. It was only the sheer immensity of the trees that was similar and that had made them seem the same.

"All these trees don't have sap, do they?" he asked.

"Of course not."

"Then why did we hide in one that did?"

"I like sap. It smells nice."

Radek glared at him, but Ovian seemed not to notice and continued to lead Radek over the branches. They moved surprisingly quickly. The peculiar makeup of the trees on this planet made the canopy a more level surface than the ground beneath them, a fact for which he was immensely grateful. They had to go around several holes, but they presented no great obstacle.

The sun had dipped beneath the horizon by the time they reached the clearing where the goblins had landed. Other than a few lights dotting the area, the makeshift landing site was dark. It gave Radek hope that it was sparsely populated and easy to sneak into. Ovian sang a few words and a vine lowered them down, and they continued on the ground. They kept an eye out for scouts but they didn't find any.

"I would think a warlike race would keep better watch," Radek whispered.

"They must be on the nova dragon. They probably don't care about these ships anymore."

"What about the ones that were chasing us?"

"We moved faster than them. Come on. Let's find a ship before anyone gets here."

They avoided the larger ships as they had no way to deal with the internal defenses. It only took them a few minutes to find a fighter like the one they'd arrived in. This time, the vessel powered up as soon as Radek tapped the screen. He worked the switches until the ship lifted off the ground. There was a commotion as goblins ran out of the larger ships and surrounded them, but he tilted the control stick back and pushed it forward. The fighter shot into the sky. He wasn't sure when they left the atmosphere, but a few seconds later, the huge shape of the nova dragon came into visual range, its ax-like shape dominating their field of view. The fighter's sensors went off, indicating they'd been targeted by the warship.

Radek looked over his shoulder at Ovian. "We really need to start thinking our ideas all the way through."

CHAPTER 33

R adek pushed forward on the control stick, and the fighter shot under the nova dragon. He tilted the ship so it was headed toward the bigger vessel and held down the firing control. A brilliant beam of purple light shot forward and splashed against a field of yellow energy. The shield barely seemed to ripple. He let out a breath. So much for the shield's power being consumed by burning through the soil. Still, even if he'd gotten through the shield, a vessel like their fighter was little more than an insect buzzing around a bear. There was no way they could damage it.

"Stay close," Ovian said. "I'm not sure it can lock on to us if we're right next to it."

"Right," Radek said. "Any idea about what else we do?"

"Keep shooting?"

Radek fired another blast but to no greater affect than the first. They reached the back of the ship and immediately turned around and fired again.

"We can't just keep doing this." The console beeped, and he glanced at the proximity detector. "Ships are coming up from the planet. Staying close won't work if others can fire on us too."

"Let's head to Droshala to warn the elves."

Radek nodded and switched to the navigation screen. He started inputting the coordinates to the elven homeworld, but stopped. He'd forgotten about the goblin numbering system. The fighter rocked as a laser blast hit the ship. It was only a glancing blow, but the proximity detector showed half a dozen fighters approaching as well as a couple of larger ships. He ran through the equations in his head, but another blast made him lose his place, and he had to start again.

"Anytime now," Ovian said.

"I'm trying. If you knew more about math, you could help."

"There are buttons back here too. Maybe I have access to the weapons."

"Try it," Radek said as he spun the ship around.

He tapped the weapon control, releasing a series of smaller bursts. A few of them hit one of the approaching fighters. The first burst washed over a bubble of purple energy. The next few impacted directly on the ship, though it kept coming. "You seem to be getting good at that," Ovian said.

"Did you figure anything out yet?"

There was the sound of buttons being mashed. "No, I don't think my console is activated. Can you turn it on?"

Radek examined the switches, but most of them still escaped his grasp. Two other ships appeared before him, and he swerved away, firing a few blasts at the nova dragon above them. He tried running the calculations again, but his focus was drawn to the ships firing on them, and he dipped to avoid another blast.

"I can't keep this up much longer."

"Then let's go."

"I can't make the calculations."

"Then don't go to Droshala. Go somewhere we can hide until you can figure it out."

Radek nodded. He still remembered the coordinates for Halune. If he altered those just a little, he could make a short jump. Hopefully, the goblins wouldn't know where he went. He punched the coordinates into the navigation system, altering the last number slightly. He hesitated for a moment, unsure in what direction he was going, but the targeting alarm went off again. He held his breath and activated the bone drive. Space flashed white for a second, and when it returned to normal, alarms blared. The shield, which was normally only visible when it was repelling an attack, suddenly became a translucent shell. Halune's sun shone brightly beneath them, its surface stretching out as far as they could see. A wide swath of red covered the bottom half of the proximity detector, and it was growing. Radek gasped as he realized they were being pulled in.

He tilted the control stick and pushed forward. The fighter struggled against the gravity, stopping their descent, but they didn't gain any altitude. He tilted the stick as far as it would go, and the fighter rotated away from the sun until they were pointed directly away from it. Slowly, the ship pulled away. They were both sweating, and their shield was only holding back a small amount of heat and radiation. Radek didn't have to translate the numbers on the indicators to know they were at dangerous levels. What little remained of his robes were soaked in sweat, and he jumped when something touched his shoulder, but it was only Ovian's hand.

The elf started singing, and gradually, Radek cooled down. The indicators remained the same, but Ovian's song served as a better protection than the shields. They were just pulling free of the sun's gravity well when another fighter appeared in front of them, no more than a quarter mile away. Radek glanced at the proximity detector, but it showed nothing. Radek eased back on the control stick until the force of the engines equaled the gravity of the star, rendering them motionless. Ovian stopped his song, though by that point, the shields did an adequate job of protecting them.

"I don't think they can see us," Radek said. "It looks like the star's radiation is interfering with their sensors."

"But we're close enough that they should be able to see us without sensors."

"Maybe if we weren't directly in front of the sun," Radek said. "We should just stay here until they go away."

At that moment, one of the status lights turned red. Radek glanced at it, and his blood went cold. It was the engine. They constant struggling against the sun's gravity was too much.

"I think the engine is about to give out."

"The weapons are still working, aren't they?"

"Yes."

"There's only one fighter, and they don't know we're here. Maybe you can destroy them."

Radek nodded and tilted their fighter until they were pointed directly at the other one. The targeting system didn't work this close to the sun, but he was reasonably sure he could hit them. His hand hovered over the firing control, afraid he would miss. It was only when Radek noticed a slight blue flicker in the engine status indicator that he took in a deep breath and fired. The ray seemed transparent and weak. He scored a direct hit, but it barely activated the shield. The fighter turned toward them. The goblin's weapons were at full strength and their own shield only held back the blast for a second. It slammed into their ship and immediately half the lights went to blue. The force of the impact sent them flying back into the sun's gravity well, turning end over end. Radek tilted the control stick trying to stabilize them, but it had no effect. The sun continued to grow every time they faced it.

"Can that song of yours protect us from the heat of a sun?"

"No," Ovian said. "Not even close."

Ovian put a hand on Radek's shoulder. He started singing louder than Radek had ever heard before. The heat shed off him. The ship's alarms screamed and the displays showed a series of numbers, though they changed before Radek could tell what they were. Suddenly, the nose of the ship tore free. Most of the status indicators went dark. Radek felt himself being pulled apart as the tidal forces of the sun ripped at him. The tone of Ovian's song shifted. Radek could feel its power flowing through him, but it just wasn't enough. Every system in the ship went offline as it tore in half. Somehow, Ovian kept a hand on Radek's shoulder and continued singing, but the heat was too much. Radek tried to cry out, but there was no air to carry his voice. The last thing he felt was another presence envelope him, huge and incomprehensible. Then, everything went dark.

CHAPTER 34

Before he even opened his eyes, Radek noticed the ground was cold. He hadn't expected to wake up at all, and he'd certainly never thought he'd ever feel anything cold, not when he'd been so close to a sun. He opened his eyes, but the light was so bright he immediately shut them again. He turned away from the light source and opened his eyes again. The gold wall provided a near perfect reflection of the light, but he managed to look around a bit as his eyes adjusted. The entire room was plated in gold. Even the floor was covered in it. The metal had been polished so it looked like a mirror. The light seemed to be coming from a bar of shining gold hanging from a ceiling that had to be at least a hundred feet up. Ovian stirred next to him, and Radek sat up. He paused. The movement hadn't hurt at all. He looked down at himself. Instead of the tattered robes, he wore a bright red coat and a white shirt that wouldn't have been out of place in a king's court in ancient Earth. Full feeling had returned to the left half of his body.

Ovian blinked several times as he examined the room. Droshala's sun was brighter than earth's, so he adjusted to the brightness more quickly. Finally, his eyes fell on Radek.

"Where are we?"

"I have no idea. I thought we were dead."

"Me too," Ovian said.

Radek pointed to an area along the wall. "I think that's a door."

Ovian nodded and they walked toward it. As Radek reached forward to see if he could find some sort of access panel, the door slid upward, and they stepped into a long corridor.

"Have you ever seen anything like this?"

Ovian bent down and picked up a gold coin that had been lying on the floor. He turned it over in his hand. Both sides were worn, but on one, Radek could barely make out the image of a cross. On the other, there was a shape that could've been a shield. Ovian shook his head. He moved to put the coin in his pocket, but shuddered and replaced it on the ground.

The wall of the corridor they were walking in seemed perfectly smooth. Radek ran his hand along it for several steps. His reflection on the wall, perfect aside from the yellow tinge, mirrored the motion. The wall felt like glass and had that peculiar sense of coldness. They walked for a long time, neither wanting to break the silence. A couple of times, Radek felt like they should stop, but a longing burned within him to continue, and he didn't dare slow.

Without knowing why, he placed his hand on a panel, and a door slid open. They looked inside and found heaps of gold and silver coins reaching halfway up to a ceiling that was barely visible. Every one had been polished to the point where they practically shone. Radek and Ovian entered the room in awe of the wealth. It wasn't just coins. Marble statues dotted the cavernous room and jewel encrusts swords and other weapons lay scattered around. Metallic chests were filled to the brim with gems of every kind. Ovian walked to one and picked up a ruby as big as his hand. He hummed for a few seconds and his eyes went wide.

"This ruby is perfect."

Radek shook his head. "I don't think you should be touching anything. We don't know who those belong to."

"You don't understand," Ovian said without taking his eyes from the gem. "It's perfect, even down to a molecular level. My people say that an entire planet might only have one perfect gem on it, one that could hold half a dozen enchantments. Most worlds don't have a single one. Even the gems we call perfect are only shadows to this one. It could hold at least fifty, or it could hold one for years, maybe even decades. You could search a dozen planets and only find one like this. One, if you're lucky." He ran his fingers through the other gems. "They're all perfect. This is incredible."

"Ovian, leave them."

"But..."

"Leave them. I doubt we're alone here."

Ovian stared at the gems for several seconds before replacing the ruby. With a visible effort, he turned away and rejoined Radek at the center of the room. They walked forward, with Ovian keeping his eyes focused straight ahead, not willing to examine the treasure anymore. They exited the room through a door on the other side and entered a sprawling cavern. As soon as the door slid shut behind them, lights scattered across the ceiling came to life, and the creature that had been slumbering at the other end stirred.

The scaled figure lifted its head and stared at them. Its blood red scales shimmered in the ambient light of the room. Its long serpentine tale wound around the chamber, and a reptilian head atop a long neck moved toward them. The creature's eyes were like fire that made those that had been on the golem seem dim. It showed its teeth and a forked tong flickered out. A small curl of smoke rose from its mouth. It unfolded its wings and spread them into a span that went at least three hundred feet. Radek took a step back and bumped into Ovian. The elf was staring at the creature, completely frozen.

The dragon opened its mouth revealing teeth as big as Radek's head, and he was sure it was going to eat them. Instead, it laughed.

CHAPTER 35

The dragon's laughter shook the room. Scattered coins rattled on the ground, and Radek could feel the deep rumbling in his bones. It was so loud it should've hurt his ears, but for some reason, it didn't. He stared up at the creature the likes of which hadn't been seen on Earth for over a thousand years. Though it was only a little bigger than the golem, the sense of it was completely different. This was fear and power given form. He could understand how ancient armies could be destroyed coming against a creature like this.

"Calm yourselves, little ones," it said in fluent elven. It sniffed at the air, and Radek felt a faint brushing against his mind. "I couldn't be sure before you woke, but I was right. A human. Has your race finally joined the rest of us among the stars?"

"Yes." His voice came out in a squeak, and he realized he'd switched to English.

The dragon smiled and also spoke in that language. "Now, I haven't heard this tongue spoken by a living being in a few thousand years."

Radek took a step back. "You speak it very well."

The dragon chuckled. "You're people piqued my interest when

you started launching artificial satellites. Purely technological. It was very impressive. No other race has managed a similar feat." He raised a clawed hand at one wall and English words started scrolling across it. It took Radek a second to recognize it as news from Earth about the new war with the goblins. The dragon gave Radek a toothy grin that sent chills down his spine. "I monitored your communications. I always suspected your kind would have a great impact on the galaxy when you finally rediscovered the primal forces of the universe. After a hundred years or so, I got tired of waiting."

"Umm, sorry about that."

The dragon blinked at him before letting out a chuckle. When she spoke, Radek could still hear the laughter in her voice. "It took me a while to understand your language. It had changed much since I left Earth. Since you started launching satellites, it would seem changes to your speech have been minimal. It's not unexpected once a world achieves global communication. Language stabilizes."

"What are you saying?" Ovian asked.

"Oh, I'm sorry, little elf," the dragon said, switching back to Elven. "It's been so long since I've had visitors that I seem to have forgotten the courtesies. I was fascinated by the human." He went back to English. "Would you mind terribly if we spoke in Elven so your friend can understand."

"No," Radek said in Elven. "That's fine."

"Wonderful!"

"Does this mean you're not going to eat us?"

"Eat you? Why in the stars would I eat you?" The chamber rumbled as the dragon laughed. "Oh, I admit I used to do that, but that was so long ago I'm surprised your kind even remembers, and in my defense, it was mainly those who came into the lands I had claimed for myself. No, I'm not going to eat you. I have often longed for the taste of human, but stellar matter provides more than enough to meet my needs."

Radek's mouth went dry. "Well, that's...good."

"Stellar matter?" Ovian asked. "You eat stars?"

Again, the dragon laughed. "Don't look so surprised. Our natural immunity to heat and radiation makes it fairly easy."

Radek looked around. He tried to find the source of the ambient light, but it was coming from everywhere. There was heat too, and Radek's eyes went wide.

"Where exactly are we?"

"We're in my lair, of course."

"But where is that?"

The walls around them flared brightly for a second and Radek had to shield his eyes. He wasn't looking when the dragon answered. "Beneath the surface of the star, of course."

"Why aren't we dead?" Ovian asked.

Smoke puffed out of the dragon's nostrils. "Magic, of course. It's no different than the spells maintaining life support and inertial dampeners."

"But even with our strongest magic, we can't go into stars."

"Of course you can't. That's why we came here."

"Here?" Ovian asked. "You mean all dragons are living in this star?"

"Not this one. We don't really enjoy spending a lot of time with each other. Every dragon chose its own star to live in."

"But stars are huge. You all used to live on one planet."

"And we had no end of conflict. We decided to avoid that."

Radek looked around. "That's where you retreated to?"

"Where else?"

"I thought you left the galaxy."

The dragon lifted her head and smoke puffed out of her nostrils. She swished her tail and knocked over a pile of coins. One rolled across the ground and ran into Radek's foot. He looked up from it to see the dragon staring at him.

"Why would we leave the galaxy?" the creature asked.

"I don't know why you left in the first place."

"We left because we got tired of getting pulled into the affairs of short lived races."

"That's why you hid your ships," Ovian said with wide eyes.

"Of course. You're not ready for that kind of power."

"You're..."

Ovian let out a series of growls. Radek gaped at him, but the dragon winced.

"That's a horrible pronunciation. Call me Rania."

"I thought you were green."

The dragon looked over her body. A stream of flame flowed out of her nostrils, its reflection lit up the floor beneath her, and she stood and stretched out. Her form took up nearly half the room. "I wonder when that happened."

Radek gaped at her. "You didn't know you were red?"

The dragon let out a puff of smoke. "I haven't had visitors in a very long time. Our color is based on a variety of factors. Environment plays a heavy role. I suppose living in a star could have this effect." She let out a puff of smoke. "In fact, that makes sense. I'd guess few dragons are any color other than red anymore. In any case, that's something to consider another time. How is it you know of me?"

"We saw the logs you left on *Trakorki*."

Rania narrowed his eyes. "You found my ship? How?"

"The trees told me where it was," Ovian said.

Rania snorted. "Your people and the trees. I should've considered that. Did the golems give you any trouble?"

"Two were deactivated. One attacked us. We had to destroy it."

Rania let out a stream of smoke. "You destroyed one of my golems? Impressive."

"But the goblins got to your ship."

The dragon laid her head on the ground, the polished gold providing a near perfect reflection. "They wouldn't be able to activate its primary systems. Not without the access codes."

"But they were able to activate it. We tried to go after it."

"You went after it in that fighter? The one that was destroyed in the star's gravity well?"

"Yes."

"How is it you weren't destroyed?"

Radek glared at him. "We were."

The dragon let out a chuckle that shook the room. "Yes, I suppose you were. A ship like that wouldn't be more than a speck to a dreadnaught." Rania closed her eyes. The room shimmered for a second, and Radek's skin tingled. He thought he could hear voices, but they were so soft, he couldn't be sure. After a second, the dragon opened his eyes. "It would seem you're right. They have the ship."

"That's not the important part," Ovian said. "They're going to use that ship to attack Droshala."

"Yes, the goblins always were a warlike race. I regret that they were able to activate *Trakorki*, but there are many systems that were disabled in case one of the other races managed something like this."

"That was deliberate?"

Rania gave a toothy smile. "Even we aren't so arrogant as to believe our security is perfect. Another race finding one of our warships was always a possibility, though admittedly, we didn't expect it to happen so soon."

"Soon?" Radek asked. "Haven't you been here for thousands of years?"

"Soon is a relative concept."

Radek just stared at her for a second. "They knew where to look, though. They killed my father to make sure we wouldn't set up a colony on the world. They knew the access codes. Are you so sure they won't know how to replace the power source?"

"All viable power sources capable of powering the most dangerous weapons were hidden away."

"So were the ships," Radek said. "The goblins found those."

The dragon inclined his head in concession of the point. "True enough. The power source was hidden in a star in the Branian system."

Ovian gasped, and Radek looked at him. His friend had gone pale.

"What is it? Do you know where that system is?"

The elf nodded slowly. "They taught us the dragon name for a lot of systems. Branian is what the dragons call the star that Treya orbits. The goblins aren't heading for the elven home world. They're heading for the human colony, for..."

He looked Radek in the eye, and Radek's blood went cold. "Home."

CHAPTER 36

You have to stop them," Radek said. "Please, you can't let them get to Treya."

"I can't stop them," Rania said.

"What do you mean you can't stop them? You're a dragon. You can go into stars. You can use your magic to protect people in the vacuum of space. How could you not be able to stop them? It's only one ship."

"It's one ship created by my people. I might be able to stop and elven war ship, though even that would be a slim chance. A dragon ship, however, is an entirely different matter."

"What about communications?" Ovian asked. "Do you have a way we can contact Treya?"

The dragon shook his massive head, but then he paused and looked toward one of the walls of the cavern. "I don't, but I may have the next best thing. I didn't bring any communications equipment with me. In time, I could probably adjust my monitors, but it won't be soon enough if your suspicions are correct." Rania grinned and a small burst of flame came from between her teeth. "I have something else, though. We had many servants of the short lived races before we left. We never really built fighters for them, but

I have always enjoyed tinkering. I've spent the last hundred years putting together a prototype. It even has a communication system." In response to some unseen command, a door on the side wall slid upward. Peculiarly, this one seemed sized for humanoids. The dragon motioned with his head. "Go on."

Radek and Ovian exchanged glances before moving in the direction of the door. Radek could almost feel the dragon's eyes on them. They walked through the door and Radek's jaw dropped.

In the center of the room sat a ship unlike any he had ever seen. It was a sleek vessel. Dragon-like wings extended from a body that looked like a long drop of water. Cylindrical engines sat at the end of each wing. Radek couldn't tell what metal it was made of, but its green surface was just as reflective as the gold upon which it sat. Radek turned to look through the door to the dragon's chamber, but Rania was gone. He turned to ask Ovian a question, and gasped. The dragon was standing right behind Ovian.

"How did you do that?"

"This is my lair," Rania said as if it were the most obvious thing in the world. "I can go where I will."

"You built this?"

"Yes. The *Stellar Wind* has spectral beam weapons, compressed plasma metallic skin, self-repair mechanism, plasma beam cannon, and a modified gold drive in each wing."

"This has a dragon gold drive?" Ovian's voice was almost reverent.

"More or less. I have no way to build any other sort of drive."

"They're the fastest drive there is."

Rania chuckled. "It's true. Gold drives were faster than anything lesser races built, but like I said, it's not exactly gold. It's a gold stellar core hybrid. This ship should be twice as fast as the *Trakorki*."

"And it has communications?" Radek asked.

"Of course."

He ran up to the ship and examined it, but he saw no way to get in.

"Venushi," Rania said.

A circular panel lowered from the bottom of the ship. Radek looked at the dragon who nodded. He stepped on it, and Ovian got on next to him.

"Vani."

At the dragon's word, the hatch lifted them into the ship. There were two seats inside, set side by side. Radek sat in the one closest to the dragon, and Ovian took the other. A viewscreen was in front of them surrounded by switches and buttons. Rather than a control stick, the top of a red sphere a foot wide sat between them. As soon as they had settled into their seats, the screen between them lit up and spoke in the dragon language. Radek looked through the clear window at Rania. The dragon's face appeared on the screen and spoke several words in his native tongue. There were a series of beeping.

"Say something," the dragon said.

"What do you want me to say?" Radek asked.

"Good. Now you, Ovian."

"What?"

The ship beeped again. "Very good. I've transferred control of this ship to you. It will now respond to your voice commands. I've also changed the language to Elven so you should be able to understand all the controls. I would train you in its use, but we have no time. For now, use voice commands. The ship has a sophisticated artificial intelligence. Ask it anything about the operation of the ship, and it'll be able to answer."

Radek nodded. "How do I access communications?"

Rania's image fizzled for a second before returning against a black background. This time, it didn't match the movements of the dragon outside, and Radek realized the artificial intelligence had been based on Rania's form.

"Communications can be accessed either with a verbal command or by hitting this button." A button near the center of the control panel started blinking. "Would you like to activate communications?"

"Yes," Radek said.

The screen shifted to one asking for a destination. The voice continued. "Enter either frequency or destination name."

Radek looked at Ovian and shrugged. "Contact the governor's office on Treya."

The screen beeped. "That location is not known. Please enter coordinates."

"It was worth a try." He entered the frequency for the governor's office, the one his father had held before being reassigned to Vanel. A dark haired man with a long nose appeared on the screen. His eyes went wide. Radek smiled. Jarrend had been his father's secretary, and now he served Treya's new governor.

"Radek? Where are you? We've been trying to locate you since we got word that your father was killed. Veelan Javin said you disappeared. The elves and goblins are in all-out war."

"I know that, Jarrend," he said. "It would take too long to explain. You need to tell the governor to mobilize a defense. The goblins are on their way to Treya."

The governor's secretary stared at him. "What?"

"They have a dragon battle ship. I don't think the entire fleet would be enough to stop it, but we have to try."

"Calm down."

"I can't calm down. The goblins are going to destroy Treya if they're not stopped."

"Where did you get this information? We've been monitoring the borders ever since war broke out, and we haven't seen any indication of this."

"That's because the attack isn't coming from goblin space. It's coming from Halune."

"The planet your father was negotiating for?"

Radek let out a breath. "Yes. That's where they found the dragon ship."

"But how..."

"Look, there's no time. I don't know if they've activated the gold drive yet, but even if they haven't, they will soon. You have to get as many ships there as soon as you can."

"But..."

"Just do it. End communications."

The screen went dark.

"What happened?" Ovian asked. "Are they going to help?"

"I don't know," Radek said. "I'm not sure they believed me, but nothing I do is going to convince them. *Stellar Wind*..." He wrinkled is brow, and he spoke at the console. "That's a mouthful. Can I just call you Wind?"

"If you wish," the ship said.

Radek nodded. "Wind, let me speak to Rania."

The dragon's image appeared on the screen. "Yes? What can I do for you?"

"Can we borrow this ship? We need to get to Treya."

The dragon nodded, a decidedly strange gesture for the reptile. "Take it with my blessing. I should've done more to secure my ship against outsiders. Stop it if you can."

She uttered a series of growls, and one of the walls split down the middle from floor to ceiling. It started to open revealing a bright yellow wall of flame. Radek could barely make out the shield keeping the stellar matter out.

"Wind, can we fly through that?"

"Yes, my shields can be modulated to allow passage through the docking bay shield without dropping it."

"That's not what I meant. Can we fly through a star?"

"Stellar matter is part of my construction. I am capable of withstanding a gravity twenty times that found on the surface of this star and heat in excess of ten million..." She growled a word, and Radek looked at Ovian.

"I guess Rania didn't translate to the elven temperature scale," Ovian said. "Ten million sounds pretty high though. We should be all right."

Radek nodded. "How do I go?"

The sphere beneath the control panel illuminated. Radek hesitated for a second before placing his right hand on it. His fingers sank in, and the sphere moved to the empty space in front of Radek.

"The location of your hand on the sphere controls the rotational axis of the ship. Push the sphere forward to accelerate. Returning it to its original position will maintain a constant velocity. Pulling back will decelerate. Gold drive can be activated either verbally or with touch inputs."

Radek turned to Ovian. "What did Rania call the star Treya orbits?"

"Branian."

"Set coordinates for Branian."

The screen shifted to one displaying long range navigation. A series of numbers appeared on the bottom. "We must reach a distance of one light second from the star in order to activate the gold drive."

Radek nodded, though he wasn't entirely sure the ship would understand the gesture. He pushed the sphere forward, and they accelerated into the star.

CHAPTER 37

The ship shook slightly as they entered the star, but other than that, their flight was completely smooth. According to the sensors, the docking bay door faced the surface, so they moved forward with the ship seemingly unaffected by the matter they were flying through. After a few minutes, the fighter broke through the surface like a whale breaching the water. There was a splash of plasma, and then they were clear.

Radek scanned the proximity detector. Unlike the goblin sensors, these seemed unaffected by the stellar radiation. He saw no sign of the ship that had fired on them earlier. He tapped a button and the range of the sensors extended to cover the entire solar system. Basic readings identified Halune as a habitable world, but other than that, there was no activity in the system.

"I think they've left."

"How far have we gone?"

"Only a few thousand miles." Radek pushed the sphere forward as far as it would go, but sighed. "It'll be at least half an hour before we get far enough to engage the gold drive."

"Really?" Ovian asked. "We're going so fast."

Radek shrugged. "A light second is a long way."

"I know that. I just didn't realize it would take so long."

"I know. It's frustrating," he said. An idea struck him. "Wind, can you give us a tutorial on the basic systems."

Rania's face appeared on the screen. "Is there any system you'd like to know about?"

"Weapons," Radek said after a second. "We'll need those to stop the nova dragon."

"Primary weapon is a plasma beam cannon that fires out of the front of the ship. Each wing has a pair of high energy blasters. Both the cannon and the blaster can fire either in burst mode or continuous blast. Additionally, I am equipped with six stellar core missiles."

"You have weapons made from the core of a star?" Ovian asked.

"No, however I do possess a fabricator capable of transforming stellar plasma into missiles with a similar make up to the core of a star."

"Are you familiar with nova dragons?"

"I am not."

"Dreadnaughts," Ovian said.

The dragon vanished and was replaced by the rotating outline of a dreadnaught. Numbers and notations dotted the image. It was inside of a translucent green bubble.

"I know their defensive capabilities."

"Can you destroy one?" Radek asked.

"A dreadnaught is a capital ship. My systems are more advanced, but I'd have small chance in a head to head conflict."

"What about something that isn't head to head?"

The schematics vanished and Wind's avatar returned. "A full volley of my missiles could take down a small section of a dreadnaught's shield. A blast from the plasma beam cannon sustained for two minutes could pierce the hull. If a vital system is hit, it is possible a dreadnaught could be destroyed."

"Possible?"

"Dreadnaughts are equipped with self-repair systems of their own as well as automatic responses to hull breaches. A single fighter has approximately a one in three hundred chance."

"And we'd have to fire on the same spot continuously for two minutes?"

"Yes."

"That doesn't provide very good odds."

"One in three hundred," Wind repeated. "Confrontation with a dreadnaught is not recommended."

"But it's not a fully functional dreadnaught," Ovian said. "Remember, a lot of the systems are without power. Trakor said getting the ship unburied would use up most of the shield's energy. What can we do if the dreadnaught has no shields?"

"Without shields, the missiles could be used directly on the hull. Dreadnaughts are older than stellar core missiles and have no specific way to deal with them. There is a one in twenty chance countermeasures could be disabled. Even if that does not happen, the time necessary to maintain the cannon could be reduced by as much as ninety-five percent."

"That's something at least," Radek checked their location. They were still twenty minutes out. "Show us how to use the weapons."

For the next twenty minutes, the ship instructed them in the use of the armaments. This close to the sun, there was nothing to practice on, but Wind created sensor ghosts for them to fire at. Neither got particularly good, but they were at least adequate. Finally, the navigation screen lit up, indicating they had travelled far enough from the star to engage the gold drive. Radek tapped the button and space went white.

CHAPTER 38

They spent most of their time in hyperspace familiarizing themselves with the rest of the ship's systems. After examining the numbers, Ovian concluded the *Stellar Wind* had weapons almost as powerful as an elven war cruiser and had defensive capabilities that far exceeded any other known ship of that size. They weren't invincible, not by any means, but with their high resistance to heat and radiation, few weapons provided any serious threat unless they took massive damage.

Their legs had begun to cramp by the time they exited hyperspace, but they still made the journey in a fraction of the time it would've taken an elven vessel. Treya's white sun shone brightly in the distance. Wind's sensors detected activity on the planet below, but Radek only glanced at it to make sure no goblins had landed.

"It looks like we've beaten them here," Radek said.

"What do we do then?"

Radek looked toward the white star in the distance. "We go there. That's where Rania said the power source was hidden. Wind, take us to the star."

There was a brief flash of white as they skimmed hyperspace to make the short jump to the center of the system. The white star filled their vision, and the transparent material of the cockpit darkened to shield them from the light.

"Has it occurred to you that the dragon in that star won't be as welcoming as Rania?" Ovian asked.

"I've been trying not to think about it."

"So what do we do?"

Radek shrugged. "Wind, is there a dragon's lair in that star?"

"Yes." She let out a series of growls "makes his home in Branian."

"He has the power sources?"

"I do not have that information."

"We could always ask him," Ovian said.

"Assuming he even has a communications system. Rania didn't."

Ovian's ears twitched. "Wind, Rania didn't have a communications system either, but she spoke to us through you."

"That is correct. A dragon's mind is compatible with a transmitter powered by gold magic. I can communicate with their mind directly over short distances."

"Can you open a channel to the dragon inside?"

The image vanished and a dragon with red scales so bright they looked like they were on fire appeared on the screen. It was against a background of flames. When he saw them, he narrowed his eyes.

"Wind, is that really what he looks like?"

"Perhaps. The image is transmitted by his mind. It can be whatever he wishes."

The creature growled in the dragon language.

"I'm sorry," Radek said. "I don't understand."

Smoke streamed out of the dragon's nostrils, completely obscuring him. Only his burning blue eyes showed on the screen. He spoke again, still in the dragon tongue. Radek glanced at Ovian who looked up. Then, he smiled.

188

"Wind, can you translate?"

"Yes. His first message was 'Who are you, little ones, to think you have the right to disturb me?' The second one was 'You would dare come here and not even know how to speak with me?'"

"So he does understand us?"

"Yes," Wind said. "Most dragons speak Elven, Dwarven, Goblin, and a smattering of other languages. It is unlikely he would understand modern English though."

"Translate what I say back to him," Radek said.

"Why?" Ovian asked. "We already know he can understand us."

"Call it a hunch. Wind, start with his name. Then say, we are here to warn you. The goblins have uncovered a nova dragon." He hesitated. "Say dreadnaught, not nova dragon. They are on their way here to steal a power source from you."

The dragon's eyes glowed momentarily brighter. He spoke again and the ship's voice came on over his, delivering his words.

"So you do speak a civilized tongue. It's my task to protect our power sources from any of the short lived races. I will not permit the goblins to get one."

"Rania said she couldn't stand against a dreadnaught. Can you?" Radek paused for a second. "Wind, use Rania's actual name."

"You've met Rania?"

"She gave us this ship so we could get here ahead of the goblins. She wanted us to stop them."

"Interesting. As I recall, she piloted a dreadnaught before we retreated from the affairs of the short lived."

"Yes, it was her ship."

"I knew we should've destroyed them. No, I cannot stand against a dreadnaught. We never expected anyone to get command codes."

"But they did get them, and now the goblins are coming here."

"Come into my lair. We have much to discuss."

"Wind, can you get us in there?"

"Yes. Scanners have detected the lair, and I am receiving the frequency modulation to get through the shields."

"Take us in then."

CHAPTER 39

Wind rocked as they entered the white star. Sensors indicated a much higher density than the one Rania had inhabited. The ship slowed and diverted energy from the weapons to the engines to force its way through the stellar matter. Additional power was routed through the shields and they became an almost solid yellow bubble. After a minute, they became transparent again, and they found themselves in a large room. Unlike Rania's lair, this one seemed composed of a single chamber. It had no solid walls. Rather, the star was held back by the dragon's shield which made it impossible to tell how big the chamber was. Even the ground they landed on was like white flame. Piles of treasure big enough to fill several buildings sat in the distance and were the only things in the lair aside from the dragon itself. The creature was twice as long as Rania and seemed indistinct. Its body glowed bright orange making it seem more like fire than flesh. Its face appeared on the screen.

"Please exit your ship."

"Wind, don't translate this. We don't actually speak your language. The ship has been translating for us."

Smoke puffed out of the dragon's nostril, and when it spoke, it was in Elven without having to be translated. "Very well. I will speak in your language." Its eyes narrowed. "No, it's not your language, is it? You're human."

"Yes."

"Curious. Come out. I'll speak in the Elven tongue."

"I would not advise that," Wind said. "The temperature outside is sufficient to melt your skin and ignite your clothes."

"Can you reduce the temperature?" Radek asked the dragon.

For a moment, the creature looked surprised, but it inclined its head, and its scales dimmed. "Of course. I wasn't thinking. You should be fine now."

"Wind?"

"The temperature is still well outside of the typical comfort level of either of your races, however it provides no significant danger."

"I don't think we should ask him to cool it down any more," Ovian said. "He's still a dragon, and all the stories say they have short tempers."

Radek swallowed. "Good point. Let us out, Wind."

As soon as they were out of the ship, their robes became soaked in sweat. It was sweltering, hotter than any summer day Radek had ever experienced. He instinctively looked around for shade, but of course, there was none. He hesitated for a second before stepping off the ship's platform. He half expected to sink into the stellar fire, but the shield held him up. Still, it was difficult to pull his eyes away from the floor.

"The shield dims the light too, doesn't it?" Ovian asked.

"Yes." The dragon's rumbling voice filled the lair. "Even I wouldn't enjoy staring at a star at full brightness all the time." It glared at Radek. "Your kind had abandoned the primal forces before I left your world. I didn't expect to see one of you out here for at least another thousand years."

"Yes, they surprised us all," Ovian said, ignoring Radek's glare.

The dragon's laugh shook the chamber. Small gouts of plasma burst through the ceiling. One was long enough to brush the top of their ship, and Radek fell, fearing it would burn him, but it stopped several feet away. The dragon snorted and laid his head down on the shielded ground. Its electric blue eyes looked unblinkingly at Radek. He took a step back.

"Now, why don't you tell me about the goblins and this dreadnaught they found?"

Quickly, Radek related the events of the last couple of days. The dragon listened without interruption, though its eyes did brighten when Radek mentioned they'd destroyed a golem. When he'd finished telling his tale, the dragon stared at them for a long time. He eyed the ship.

"Rania," he stumbled a little over the name, "constructed this?"

"Yes."

"She always was impressive for one so young."

"Young? Isn't she over a thousand years old?"

The dragon blinked. "A thousand years? Has it been so long? Perhaps she's not so young after all. It's so easy to lose track."

"How old are you?"

"What year is this? Oh never mind. It doesn't really matter. Suffice to say I am the oldest dragon in existence. It was I who led us away from the affairs of other races, though I suspected we'd eventually be dragged back in."

"Sorry."

The dragon lifted his head and examined their fighter. "Very impressive." Suddenly, his head shot up and he stared into the white flame. "The goblins are here, and it seems they've brought more than a dreadnaught. There are at least six of their capital ships and several dozen lesser vessels."

The dragon got to his feet and spread his wings. They shed a light brighter than anything coming from the star. A wicked grin appeared on his face, and his eyes glowed an angry red. Radek found himself looking for a place to hide but stopped when he realized what he was doing. Ovian had taken several steps toward the ship when Radek grabbed his arm. They both turned to the dragon.

"What are you doing?" Radek asked.

Flames came from between his teeth and smoke billowed from his nostrils. The shields shimmered with every word, and Radek half expected them to fail altogether. "It's been a long time since the universe saw a dragon in battle. Get in your ship. I'll come after you. I think it's time you were reminded just what one of us can do."

CHAPTER 40

The ship surged forward as soon as they burst free of the star. The dragon came out right after them. It seized the ship in its claws and beat its wings. Space went white for a second. When it returned, Treya was directly below them. The dragon released them and flew off. Radek and Ovian exchanged glances.

"I guess dragons don't need ships to travel faster than light," Radek said.

"That is correct," Wind said. "They can't match a ship for speed, but their magic does enable them to enter hyperspace even from within the gravity well of a star."

"Show me the proximity detector."

The screen flickered and showed a concentration of dots near the planet. Radek turned the ship in that direction and accelerated. Before long, the goblin fleet had come into visual range. One ship lit up in a brilliant explosion, and when it cleared, Radek saw the dragon flying toward one of the battleships. It opened its mouth and blue-white flame shot forward, so concentrated it looked almost like a beam. It impacted the ship's shield which glowed brightly for a second before shattering. The flame crashed into the hull. The ship started to turn toward the dragon. It fired its weapons, and space came alive with energy, but it only lasted a second. The flame broke through the hull and came out the other side. The ship erupted in an explosion, taking out a few of the nearby fighters. Other ships turned toward the dragon and started firing. The dragon lifted its wings and a bright light enveloped the area, overwhelming even Radek's sensors. When it dissipated, the dragon had moved several hundred yards upward and was already diving toward the goblin fleet. Some kind of energy seemed to be leaking out of his body.

"Is he hurt?" Radek asked.

"It would appear so," Wind said.

"Are we close enough to do anything?"

"They are at the limits of the plasma beam cannon."

"Fire."

Ovian held down the firing control. A brilliant blue beam shot forward, splashing against an envelope of green energy surrounding a goblin fighter. It tried to move out of the way but Ovian kept the guns locked, and Radek pushed the sphere forward, driving them toward their target. As they approached, the goblin shields brightened. There was a flash, and the ship was gone.

Other ships were concentrating their fire on the dragon. He darted between them, spraying its deadly flame. He had already taken out two battle cruisers and several smaller vessels. Some of the ships had scattered, but they were slowly coming back to the battle, and more than one energy bean sliced into the dragon.

"Fire on any ship that's close enough!"

Ovian nodded, moving the beam from ship to ship, destroying three of them. Before long, the goblin vessels noticed them and turned to attack, but Wind's weapon range far exceeded anything goblins had ever built. Three other goblin crafts had been destroyed before they came close enough to even lock on. Balls of energy splashed against Wind's shield, but at that range, they barely had any strength at all.

"Wind, why are they having so little effect?"

Wind vanished from the screen, replaced by a status of their shields. "They are at extreme range, and their weapons are primarily heat-based, which my shields can dissipate with minimal energy loss. A single goblin fighter would have to be within a hundred yards to have a meaningful effect."

"A hundred yards?" Ovian asked. "That's it? At that rate, we could practically fight this whole battle by ourselves. "

Wind reappeared and shook his head. "A single goblin fighter would need to get that close. Multiple vessels can have a cumulative effect. Any craft heavier than a fighter would not have such a severe distance limitation."

"Got it," Radek said. "How's the dragon?"

"Wounded but alive. He is still heavily outnumbered, though not so severely as before."

"How many are coming toward us?"

"Seventeen." Another approaching fighter exploded. "Sixteen."

The impacts against the shield grew stronger. A few times, the fighter vibrated under the force of the impact. The proximity detector showed four of them as midsized cruisers. The shots coming from those were the strongest detected by the shields, and they were steadily growing stronger.

"Target those."

Ovian nodded and turned the beam toward them. "It's not working. They have stronger shields."

"Keep at it," Radek said. "It should get through once we get closer."

Suddenly, the ships in front of them vanished. The proximity detector screeched and Radek looked down at it. He gasped and turned around. The ships were directly behind them, no more than half a mile away. As one, they fired, and sixteen different energy weapons crashed against the shields. The fighter rocked, and an indicator light on the left side of the viewscreen lit up.

"Wind, what does that mean?"

"Aft shields are at twenty percent." Another blast crashed against the shield. "Eighteen percent."

Radek spun the control sphere, and the ship spun in response, its point falling and rising until they were facing in the opposite direction. Radek jammed the firing control down, and the beam sliced through the cruiser's shield. The metal glowed red and the entire thing exploded, but by then, two of the fighters had gotten behind them, firing on their weakened shield. They were so close Radek could practically reach out and touch them, and at that distance, shield strength was fading fast. If they turned, they'd expose themselves to the more powerful cruisers.

"Target the ones behind us with missiles," Radek said.

"We need those for the nova dragon."

"We need to be alive to face the nova dragon."

Ovian nodded and switched firing modes. His fingers danced across the screen, selecting targets as Radek swerved and tried to avoid the enemy blasts. After a second, Ovian hit the button. The fighter shook a little as twin balls of light shot forward. An instant later, they turned, one going left and another right. They flew behind Wind, and the two dots representing their pursuers disappeared in a flash of light. Ovian fired on another cruiser, but a fighter got between them, sacrificing itself to preserve the larger ship. The cruiser let loose missiles of its own, which crashed against Wind's shield at the same time that laser blasts struck them from the other direction. The shield shuddered. Ovian blasted a fighter out of the sky, but there were just too many.

"We can't keep this up much longer." Radek scanned the proximity detector. "There are more coming."

Ovian targeted a cruiser and fired, but Wind was rocking from the various impacts, and he couldn't keep a lock on it. The blast came out weak and the beam sputtered and died. All across the control panel, indicators flashed. The shield was losing power. It would fail any second.

Suddenly, three fighters exploded in quick succession. The rest stopped firing as half a dozen triangle shaped ships flew over them, spraying them with energy. Radek felt a smile split his face. The human fleet had arrived.

CHAPTER 41

Human ships were slow compared to their goblin counterparts, but there were more of them, and they had caught the goblins by surprise. In a matter of seconds, the ships attacking Radek had been destroyed. The sensors beeped as the human ships targeted them.

"Unknown ship," a voice said from the console. It spoke English. "Identify yourself."

"I'm Radek Almon, son of Ambassador Kenneth Almon. I'm the one that warned you about the goblin fleet."

The screen flickered and a face covered by a flight mask appeared. "Radek, the governor told us about you. What kind of ship is that? I've never seen anything like it."

"It's a dragon star fighter," Radek said.

The man sputtered for a second. "Then, can I assume that really is a dragon fighting the rest of the goblin fleet?"

Radek looked at the scanner. The dot representing the dragon was still glowing brightly. Every few seconds, another dot would blink out. Radek nodded into the screen. Still, the dragon's light was gradually dimming. It wouldn't be enough.

"We have to help him," Radek said.

"We're at least an hour away."

"Can you make a short hop like the goblins did?"

"Negative. We don't have the ability to engage the hyper drive for such short a time. We could jump out of system and jump back, but we need at least an hour between jumps for our engines to cool."

"This ship can get there faster."

"Your ship is damaged."

"Wind, what's the status?"

An outline of the *Stellar Wind* appeared on the screen. As Wind spoke different parts of the ship lit up with texts giving more details.

"Shields are at five percent. Engine coils have been burned out. Gold drive is inoperative. Weapons are at fifty percent."

"Rania said something about self-repair."

Wind's face replaced the status screen. "Yes, self-repair has been initiated. All damage is within the capability of that system."

"How long will that take?"

"Damage is extensive. Estimate full functionality in three days."

Radek's jaw dropped. "Three days?" He looked down toward the planet. Clouds swirled over green land masses. He'd never been a good student of geography and had only a vague idea of where Vayoun, the city where his grandparents lived, was. His voice was barely above a whisper. "We don't have that long."

"Repairs can be prioritized."

"Focus on the engines. Let's get there as soon as we can. Set course for the battle."

"Radek, we can't let you go," the pilot he'd been speaking to said. "You're no soldier."

"Head for the sun," Radek spoke as if the other man hadn't said anything. "We still haven't seen the battleship they found, but it needs a power source from the sun. If they get it, nothing else will matter."

Without waiting for a response, Radek pushed the control sphere forward, and they took off. At first, they moved slowly, just barely faster than a human fighter. The ship vibrated slightly and they began to pick up speed.

"Wind, how long until engines are at full power?"

"Approximately twenty minutes."

"After that, focus on shields."

"Acknowledged."

"What about defensive systems?"

"Self-repair will take a day to fully repair the shields."

"What about the missiles?"

"Missiles are at full power, but there are only three remaining."

"It's better than nothing."

Though they moved faster than any of the human ships were capable of, it still felt frustratingly slow. After fifteen minutes, half of the dots had been eliminated, each one briefly flaring in the distance. The dot representing the dragon seemed to be going dimmer. They had to be in range by now.

"Wind, can you contact him?"

The ship didn't answer, but the dragon's face appeared on the screen. Glowing blood dripped from a wound beneath its eye, and his entire image seemed hazy. Radek stared. He wondered how badly the dragon had to be hurt for an image generated by his mind to display those wounds.

"Come this way," Radek said. "We'll hold them off."

The dot turned in their directions. "A few centuries ago, I could've destroyed them all with little effort. Now, I can barely make a leap." The dot vanished and appeared several miles closer. "I will be with you soon."

"Wind, what is the status of our shield?"

"Shields are at ten percent."

"That's not a lot," Ovian said.

Radek glanced at the proximity detector. "There are only ten of them."

"We only have three missiles."

"And the rest of the weapons. They're still at half strength. That has to be better than anything they have."

The dragon flew over them. Fiery blood was flung from wounds on its wings and hit Wind, only to be evaporated by the shield. Ovian's eyes followed the creature and then turned back to the approaching ships.

"I guess we're about to find out."

"There are only four cruisers," Radek said. "Target them with the missiles."

Ovian nodded and tapped a few buttons. Glowing balls shot forward, disappearing in the distance. A few seconds later, four explosions appeared and the dots representing the cruisers went out.

"What happened?"

"The cruisers were in a tight formation. The three explosions were enough to take out the fourth one as well as a number of smaller vessels," Wind said.

Radek nodded, but Ovian was already targeting the fighters, and he fired the cannon. It took several seconds to get through the shields, but eventually, the beam broke through and the ship was destroyed. By then, the goblin ships had come close enough to use their own weapons. Their beams impacted the Wind's shields, draining their power. Ovian targeted and destroyed another one.

"Four left," Ovian said.

He switched firing modes and the blasters on the wings started firing. Another missile flew toward them, but Ovian managed to get it with their lasers. They targeted the fighters next. Two more exploded in quick succession, but the last two split up and started firing from different angles. Ovian targeted one, but their combined blasts finally broke through the dragon ship's shields. The ship rocked and sensors screeched. The one Ovian had been targeting exploded, but the other had them in its sights. Radek tried to turn, but it wouldn't be soon enough.

Suddenly, a blue white flame crashed into the fighter. It enveloped the craft, and the dot disappeared from the proximity sensor. When the flame went out, the ship was gone. Radek turned his eyes to the screen.

"Thank you," Radek said.

"You saved my life first," the dragon said.

"Have you seen the dreadnaught?"

"I have not, though without a fleet to support it, the threat will be reduced."

"Not if they get one of those power cells. Wind, scan the system. See if you can find it."

The screen beeped. "The dreadnaught has engaged the human ships."

"How are they doing?"

"They had no capital ships. Most have been disabled or destroyed."

"Can we make a micro jump to the battle?"

"Gold drive has been repaired to minimal levels. A micro jump is possible."

"All right. Let's go."

Space flashed white and Radek's throat went dry. The human fleet was in ruins. Fighters floated unpowered in space. The rubble from mid-sized cruises was strewn about. Radek scanned signals, but no one was transmitting. Some of the ships had life signs, but Radek only looked to make sure they were in no immediate danger. The proximity detector showed the dreadnaught heading toward the sun. He aimed Wind in that direction and pushed the control sphere forward as far as it would go.

"What's our status?"

"Shields are at two percent. Engines at seventy-five. Weapons at forty."

"Target the dreadnaught."

"Even without shields, I am unable to do significant damage to a dreadnaught."

"But you can do some."

"Yes."

"It's better than nothing."

CHAPTER 42

As soon as they got in range, Ovian fired. The purple beam lanced across space. For a brief instant, the shield appeared around the vessel, but the beam sliced through it. The nova dragon didn't even seem to notice the attack though, and it continued its slow plodding toward the sun.

"Wind, can you fire both the plasma beam and the blasters at the same time?"

"That cannot be done accurately."

"That thing's the size of a mountain! Are you telling me you can't hit it?"

Wind actually seemed embarrassed as she nodded. "I can hit the dreadnaught with all available weapons though targeting a specific area will be difficult."

"Then fire."

Space lit up with all the weapons unloading at once. The points of impact all hit an area of about a hundred yards, and slowly, that area began to glow. Before Radek could celebrate, however, the ship disappeared.

"The dreadnaught has engaged the gold drive and has undergone a micro jump," Wind said.

"Follow it!"

The sky flashed white and suddenly, the sun loomed big in their field of vision. They hadn't come in as close as the nova dragon, and Radek cried out as the other ship dove into the star with a splash of plasma. Slowly, it began to sink in. Radek pushed the control sphere forward.

"I would advise against this action," the ship said.

"We have to stop them!"

"Without shields, I won't survive going deep enough through the denser matter of this star to reach the lair."

"But they can?"

"Dreadnaughts have a much stronger hull than smaller ships."

"We'll just have to get them when they come out," Ovian said.

"When they come out, they'll have a fully powered ship. We won't even be able to get through their shield."

"The ship said we can make new missiles."

"Yes," Wind said, "with stellar matter, new missiles can be constructed."

"Well, there's a star right there."

"But we can't go in it," Radek said.

"That is not precisely correct," Wind said. "I cannot reach the lair, but I can dive shallowly into the star, enough to retrieve matter to construct missiles."

"How long will that take?"

"Fifty seven minutes for each missile once the matter is gathered, though I can only hold enough raw matter to construct one missile at a time."

"Fine. Let's do that. Focus auto repair on the plasma beam cannon. I want it as strong as possible when they come out."

"But the shields..." Ovian's said.

Radek shook his head. "That thing is too powerful. We're not going to get the shields strong enough to make any difference."

Ovian nodded and the ship dove into the sun. Without an active shield, the pair had to guard their eyes, and Wind shook violently for several minutes before it pulled out. A progress bar appeared showing how much of the missile was complete and it started slowly creeping across the screen. Radek kept his eyes locked on the sensors. They couldn't scan the interior of the star, but he stayed vigilant for any sign of the nova dragon emerging. The missile was only halfway complete when the surface of the sun began to boil. The nova dragon emerged, its shields shining brightly. Ovian turned to Radek who gaped.

"I have no idea what to do."

The ship flew past them, trailing stellar matter that splashed against their hull. It took a few seconds for Wind to stabilize."

"It's like it didn't even see us," Ovian said.

"I have engaged defensive measures that render us invisible to *Trakorki*'s scanners," Wind said.

"You can do that?"

"Not for most ships, but the dragon who built me is the same one who commanded that ship. The goblins have not yet changed the command codes."

They had to stop the nova dragon, but they just didn't have the power. At least they didn't if they struck from the outside.

"You have the ship's command codes?"

"Yes, that is correct."

"How about for the shields?"

"I cannot drop the shields, if that's what you are asking."

Radek shook his head. He hadn't thought of that. "It's not. You got us through the shields in Rania's lair."

"Yes. I understand. I can get through *Trakorki*'s shields."

"Great," Ovian said. "We can get inside the shields and start firing. Maybe we can destroy the ship."

"That wouldn't work," Radek said. "We're nowhere near strong enough, even once the missile is complete."

"That is correct," the ship said. "The explosion of a stellar core missile will produce a significant amount of damage, though it would not cripple a fully functional dreadnaught. Even if we survive the blast, it is likely we would be detected."

"Then, what do you have in mind?"

"How long before they can jump?" Radek asked.

"Perhaps one hour before they escape the sun's gravity well."

"Do you know where the gold drive is?"

"Yes."

"Is there a hall near it close to the hull?"

"How close?"

"Close enough that we can break through the hull if we set a collision course."

"You want to ram the ship?" Ovian asked. "Diving into a star didn't destroy it. Do you really think we can?"

"I'm not trying to destroy it, at least not by ramming it. I just want to get inside."

A schematic of the nova dragon appeared on the screen. A red dot flashed near the back. "I can go through the hull here. That will put you fifty yards from the gold drive chamber. You will be detected, though."

"At this point, I really don't care. With a little luck, they won't be able to catch us before we go to the drive room."

"Sensors detect three dozen goblins on the ship, split between the bridge and the various weapons chambers. None are within two hundred yards of the gold drive."

"That'll be the plan then. Target that area."

The ship rotated and beeped in acknowledgement, and Radek pushed forward on the control sphere. They shot forward. Radek couldn't help but brace himself as they passed through the shields, but the energy barrier had no effect. He closed his eyes as the star fighter rammed into the nova dragon.

CHAPTER 43

There was a crushing sound as the star fighter's sleek form pierced the hull of the nova dragon. Alarms sounded and indicators went dark as the fighter's engines drove them deeper into the ship. Inertial dampeners went offline, and Radek and Ovian were driven back into the chairs with such forced that Radek almost blacked out. Finally, they crashed through a wall and ground to a stop in the middle of a hall. The corridor to the left had collapsed, but down the right one, a faint yellow light pulsed.

"I have used my shield to plug the hole we made," Wind's voice seemed far away and there was a whirring sound as he spoke. "You will have atmosphere outside, but it will not last long. You should hurry. Sensors detect the goblins are on their way."

Radek nodded and Wind lowered them down. The air was hot outside, and the smell of fried circuits filled the air. Radek hoped they belonged to the nova dragon and not the *Stellar Wind*, but smoke billowed from the fighter. Its nose had been bent and a long swath of metal had been melted in the hull near the cockpit. Radek worried it wouldn't be able to fly. He could see his worries mirrored on Ovian's face, but neither said anything, and they dashed down the hall. As they approached the room with the yellow light, Radek felt tingling on his skin. It kept getting stronger until they reached the doorway and entered the room that was the source of what he was feeling.

The thing in the center of the room looked like a jumble of golden wires. There had to be hundreds of them coming together to form an almost solid mass in the center. The formation in the center seemed to be round one instant and more like a cube in the next, though with so many wires, Radek couldn't be sure it wasn't just some trick of the light. They stared at it for several seconds, not quite able to believe what they were finally seeing. It was a dragon gold drive.

"So what do we do now?" Ovian asked.

"We wreck it. We pull apart the wires."

Ovian gaped at him. "Are you serious?"

"What? Do you have a better idea?"

Ovian shook his head. "You really don't have any idea at all do you? Did you even listen when they tried to teach you about magic? That won't work. You can't just pull apart something that complicated. Only part of it is bound to the physical form."

"Fine. Give me a crystal. I'll blow it up like I did with the golem."

"I don't have one."

"Can you sing at it?"

Ovian stared at him for several seconds before closing his eyes. He started to sing, but nothing happened. After a moment, he shook his head. "It's shielded, just like the conduits."

"We have to do something," Radek said. "We came all this way. We can't just fail now."

"The goblins will be here any second."

Radek let out a breath. After a second, he lifted his voice. "Trakor, are you here?"

The transparent blue image appeared on the screen. When it saw them, its eyes widened, and its gaze wandered from the gold drive back to them. The image flickered for a few seconds before speaking.

"You're back."

"Yes. Are the goblins on their way here?"

"I detected a breech, and they went to investigate. They found a small vessel lodged in my hull. They tried to remove it, but it engaged defenses and drove them off." He paused for a second. "They are coming this way."

"Can you seal the door?"

"Sealing the door requires access to secondary commands."

"Can you contact the ship in your hull?" The screen went dark for a second. When it returned, Trakor was shaking his head. "It is not responding to hails."

"Tell him Radek wants him to respond."

There was a beep. "It is responding."

"Patch me through. Wind, give Trakor the command codes to its systems."

There were several beeps and the door to their chamber slid shut.

"The door has been sealed."

"But they'll be able to open it again?"

"Yes, they have entered command codes as well."

"Change them," Ovian said.

"What?"

"Wind said he could pass through the shields because the goblins never bothered to change the command codes. Can you change them?"

Radek looked at the ship's avatar. "Can I?"

"Yes."

"Change the command codes to..." he hesitated for a second. "Seven."

The screen beeped in acknowledgement. Ovian raised an eyebrow.

"Seven? That's it?"

"It'll keep them out for now. Trakor, does the ship have a self-destruct?"

"Power has not been restored to that system."

There was a bang on the door and an orange glow appeared in the center, filling the room with an acrid scent. The air around the door was distorted by heat. Radek and Ovian exchanged glances.

"Trakor, what's going on?"

"They are firing their weapons at the door. They will burn through in a few minutes."

Radek ran to the gold drive and shoved his hands into the wires. Instantly, power ran through him, and he felt his hair stand on end. He could sense the power, and his mind reeled at it. It was unimaginably complex. Lines of energy ran through the wires and leapt between them. They formed a pattern he could study for years and not begin to understand. He pulled at it, and for just a moment, he held it. Burning heat filled his body. He clenched his teeth and moved one strand of power before the pressure of it against his thoughts became too much. His mind couldn't grasp it, and the power fell back onto the drive with such force the wires vibrated. Radek doubled over, breathing heavily. It felt like a stake had been driven through his head.

"I can't do it." The glow on the door grew wider, and Radek's eyes widened as an idea struck him. He took Ovian's hand. "Sing the song that lets us breathe in space." Ovian gave him a questioning look but Radek glared at him, and the elf started to sing. "Wind, drop your shields. Lower your access hatch, and be ready to catch us. Trakor, open the door."

Ovian's eyes bulged, but he kept singing. A second later, the door slid open. Goblins cried out, but their calls faded. Radek yelped as he was sucked into the hall with Ovian right behind him. They flew toward Wind, and Radek could see goblins floating in empty space beyond. As soon as they passed under the fighter, its shields reactivated, sealing in the atmosphere. Radek and Ovian fell to the ground. They slid against the energy bubble and came to a stop.

"Come on." Radek got into the access hatch.

"But we haven't done anything."

"We will. Come on." Ovian joined him on the hatch. They were raised up into the ship, and took their seats. "Wind, can you take off?"

"Engines are offline."

Radek sighed. "Yeah, that would've been too much to hope for. Is the missile ready?"

"It is."

"Radek, we barely have shields," Ovian said. "If you fire that while we're lodged in here, there's no way we'll survive."

"We might, if we get blown free. It's our best chance, unless you have a better idea."

Ovian's jaw dropped. For a moment, Radek thought he was going to argue some more, but a smile appeared on his face.

"No, not really."

Radek grinned, but both of their faces went somber. Ovian held his finger suspended over the fire control. Radek tried to swallow the lump that formed in his throat. He'd broken out in a cold sweat, and Ovian was breathing heavily.

"We can't let the goblins have that ship," Radek said.

Ovian gave him one slow nod and pressed the button. Wind lurched back as the missile streaked down the hall and exploded as it hit a wall. Flame rushed toward them. The nova dragon shook, and the shield around the *Stellar Wind* flickered and failed. The force of the explosion tore them free and set them spinning. Radek felt like he was going to sick up as the fighter turned end over end. Ovian started to sing, and gradually, the ship slowed and came to a stop, facing the nova dragon as the war ship lumbered away from them. Smoke billowed from the hole, but otherwise, the larger ship seemed undamaged. Radek shook his head in disbelief. After all that, they had failed, completely.

"Wind," he said in a voice barely above a whisper. "Can you scan it?"

"Yes. The gold drive is undamaged. Internal suppression mitigated the explosion. They still can't see us, but we didn't stop them."

"Then let's go after them."

"While the dreadnaught is largely undamaged, I cannot say the same about myself. Engines are down. So are shields and weapons. Sensors are operating at minimal power, and my program will likely fail any minute. It's taking everything else I have to keep life support and camouflage activated. We're dead in space."

Tears welled up in Radek's eyes. It was over. The goblins would descend on the galaxy with their unstoppable ship. Unless the other races formed a cohesive defense, no one would be able to stand against them. The goblins would conquer whatever they could and destroy the rest, all because he and Ovian had failed.

"How long until they're out of the sun's gravity well?" he asked.

"They should be able to jump any second now."

Suddenly, the smoke coming for the nova dragon stopped. A brilliant yellow light shone from the hole, and cracks spidered across the hull. Wind's sensors screeched and the entire warship began to glow.

"Wind, what's going on?"

Before the ship could answer, the nova dragon exploded. An

energy wave passed over them, and the console of the fighter cracked, spewing electricity at Radek. Pain surged through him. He cried out once before falling into unconsciousness.

CHAPTER 44

Radek awoke to a sterile scent. He opened his eyes. He was in a white room, lying in a bed he didn't recognize. A viewscreen hung on the wall, but it wasn't active. The dim white sun shone through the window. He tried to sit up and pain shot through his body. There was a beep and a few seconds later a woman in healer's robes came in. She waved a wand over him and chanted for a few seconds. Radek's ability with human magic was no greater than its elven counterpart, and the words refused to stick in his memory. The pain receded though.

"Where am I?"

"You're in the Yellow Sea Medical Center."

Radek blinked and struggled to understand the words. The city of Vayoun was on the shores of the Yellow Sea. "I'm on Treya?"

She ran a hand scanner over him and examined the readout. "Yes. One of the cruisers picked up your fighter and brought you here. There are a lot of people anxious to speak to you, if you're feeling up to it."

Radek nodded and sat up. The pain no longer bothered him, and the healer poked her head into the hall. A few seconds later, a tall man with pale eyes and a woman with a round face walked in. Their hair was more white than grey, and relief was painted on their faces. As soon as Radek saw them, tears welled in his eyes, and he looked away from them.

"Grandma. Grandpa. Dad is dead."

The next thing he knew, they were all embracing. They'd heard, of course. The message Ovian's father sent had gotten through long ago, but by the time they got it, he and Ovian had already snuck onto the goblin ship. He started telling them about what had happened, but he had to stop several times. Those memories held a great deal of pain. Somehow, he got through the story. About halfway through, a man in a military uniform came in. Radek knew he should be able to tell his rank by the decorations he wore, but his mind still felt scrambled.

"Is Ovian all right?" he asked once he was done with the tale.

As if in response, Ovian walked in. He was favoring one leg and he wore a bandage on his forehead, but otherwise, he seemed well. Radek smiled.

"He wasn't hurt as bad as you were," the man said as he extended a hand. "I am General Vadreen. That's quite a ship you have there. Your friend tells me it's already repaired some of its own systems."

Ovian nodded. "Wind said she still needs raw materials." He glared at the general. "They wanted to take her, but Wind wouldn't let them."

"It's the most advance piece of technology we've ever seen," Vadreen said. "It has to be studied."

"Maybe we can get plans from it," Radek said, "but the ship is ours. A dragon gave it to us."

"But you're only children," the general said.

"Children who saved this world," Radek's grandfather pointed out, "and quite possibly the galaxy along with it."

Radek blinked at them. "How exactly did we do that?"

"Wind explained it to me," Ovian said. "It got readings as the nova dragon blew up. The magic in the gold drive had been altered. There's too much energy running through those things, and even a small change to the spells on them can be catastrophic. That's why it was shielded against my magic. Apparently, it wasn't against yours."

"Mine?"

"Dragons left known space before humans developed interstellar drives. Defense against human magic was never developed. You did it when you tried to change it. Wind is sure of it."

The general sighed. "We can't force you to let us study it." He chuckled. "There are some who would like to try, but it's too powerful and too able to defend itself. The ship is yours."

Ovian's eyes darted around. "Finally. Now, if we can just get her the raw materials she needs, we can go back to *Vanel.*"

Radek blinked at him. "We're going back?"

"Of course. I already spoke to my father. He's mad, but he'll let you return. I think Rania had something to do with it."

"Rania?"

"Yeah, she went to the station. The dragons are coming back to space, and they want us to be ambassadors. My father's not happy, but the dragons won't accept anyone else. Isn't that great? I'm going to be a Veelan at the same time as my father."

In spite of himself, Radek laughed.

ABOUT THE AUTHOR

Gama Ray Martinez lives near Salt Lake City, Utah. He moved there solely because he likes mountains. He collects weapons in case he ever needs to supply a medieval battalion, and he greatly resents when work or other real life things get in the way of writing. He secretly hopes to one day slay a dragon in single combat and doesn't believe in letting pesky things like reality get in the way of his dreams. Find him at http://gamarayburst.com/ as well as http://www.facebook.com/gamarayburst

Made in United States
Troutdale, OR
09/30/2023

13310694R00142